Y0-BPV-966

"You make me crazy, Anne," James whispered.

"I don't want to," she said breathlessly.

His hand reached out, his fingers lightly tracing her cheek. She felt as if she were being burned, yet she couldn't pull away.

"You make me more than crazy," he said, moving closer, so close that darkness seemed to envelope them like a cocoon.

"Don't," she said when his body pressed against hers, making her ache.

"Don't what?" he asked, his hand curving around her throat in a gentle caress. Her skin felt like silk under his fingers.

"Don't do this. Don't kiss me like you did before," she begged.

"I'll kiss you better," he promised.

His mouth covered hers. She knew she should pull away, walk away, run away. But she was already tumbling off a cliff and into a sensual fire she'd known only once before—in James Farraday's arms. . . .

WHAT ARE *LOVESWEPT* ROMANCES?

They are stories of true romance and touching emotion. We believe those two very important ingredients are constants in our highly sensual and very believable stories in the *LOVESWEPT* line. Our goal is to give you, the reader, stories of consistently high quality that may sometimes make you laugh, sometimes make you cry, but are always fresh and creative and contain many delightful surprises within their pages.

Most romance fans read an enormous number of books. Those they truly love, they keep. Others may be traded with friends and soon forgotten. We hope that each *LOVESWEPT* romance will be a treasure—a "keeper." We will always try to publish

LOVE STORIES YOU'LL NEVER FORGET
BY AUTHORS YOU'LL ALWAYS REMEMBER

The Editors

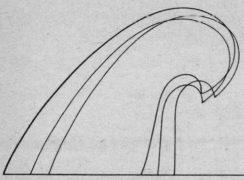

LOVESWEPT® • 367

Linda Cajio
Unforgettable

BANTAM BOOKS
NEW YORK • TORONTO • LONDON • SYDNEY • AUCKLAND

For Colleen, who
likes Lettice as much
as I do.

UNFORGETTABLE

A Bantam Book / December 1989

*If you would be interested in receiving protective vinyl
covers for your Loveswept books, please write to this address
for information:*

*Loveswept
Bantam Books
P.O. Box 985
Hicksville, NY 11802*

ISBN 0-553-44004-7

Published simultaneously in the United States and Canada

PRINTED IN THE UNITED STATES OF AMERICA

O   0 9 8 7 6 5 4 3 2 1

One

He was perfect.

Anne Kitteridge forced the army of sensual butterflies in her stomach to calm as she watched the man on the sleek polo pony. The polo game had been fast and furious for three quarters, and despite the cool spring day, his white knit shirt was plastered to his body, outlining every muscle of his shoulders and back. They led into a flat waist and narrow hips. Strong thighs bulged as he gripped the sides of the galloping bay gelding. The strength in his arms was obvious, and she had an unwanted urge to feel them around her in a tight embrace. Intent on the ball, he kept his lean six-foot frame crouched low on the animal's shoulders. She knew the polo helmet hid thick, light brown hair, vivid green eyes, a Robert Redford jaw, and a Cary Grant smile.

He rode hard past her on a drive to the goal, and she drew in her breath when he rose out of the saddle to hit the ball. He had a perfect backside too.

If only she hadn't seen James Farraday on a horse, she thought, sighing. He was thirty-five, single, and from one of Philadelphia's foremost families. Playboy material. She had known him all her life, although she had seen him only occasionally since her return from California five years before. She went out of her way to keep their meetings to a minimum. But his grandmother and hers were close friends, and when she and James were children, the families had hoped they would marry someday. . . .

Anne swallowed. She hadn't allowed herself to think of that in years. Not since she was seventeen when she had made a fool of herself with him. Then she'd proceeded to make a mess of her life. She was all grown up now—grown up and grown sensible.

It was just the horses, she told herself. Horses were her territory, after all. She had been riding since she could walk; she'd even ridden for a time as a professional jockey. Now she bred race horses for a living. Somehow, though, she hadn't quite connected that an ability to play polo meant an ability with horses. She knew all too well that at this moment James's senses were filled with pounding hooves, musky sweat, and hot leather. She knew he was moving with the horse in that unique, almost telepathic affinity between man and equine. She knew his brain and body were absorbed in nature, racing toward contented exhaustion. A throbbing started deep within her and radiated outward until she felt as if she were melding with him on the animal—urging him forward, harder and faster . . .

As if he had sensed her thoughts, James glanced around at the spectators crowding the sidelines of the Westgate Country Club's charity polo match. She instantly turned away before his gaze found hers, mortified that she might have somehow signaled her reaction to him.

She reminded herself she had an intense distrust of "perfection." And for her own good, it had to stay that way. Really, she thought in disgust, she was a thirty-one-year-old single mother and businesswoman. Much too old for such a silly adolescent reaction to a man.

This was the first and last time her grandmother would talk her into attending a tailgate party/polo game, Anne decided. Usually she was more resistant to the social functions Lettice wanted her to attend, but she hadn't been to one for a while. This one had horses, and she'd allowed Lettice to prevail. Horses . . . and James. She slipped her arms out of her collarless green tweed jacket. Funny, she mused, how the March day turned quite warm suddenly. Her yellow linen shirtwaist even seemed too heavy.

Across the small table from her, Lettice Kitteridge lowered her binoculars and smiled with satisfaction. "James is in top form. Very top form."

Lord, Anne thought with amusement. He even had her grandmother drooling. No mean feat, if one knew Lettice. But James probably had every woman there panting. He usually did.

She glanced over at the furious play farther down the field, then shrugged as nonchalantly as possible. At least she could show a natural interest in the other players.

"He's got a wonderful horse," she said, pleased with her casual tone. Her insides were still pulsing with heat. "His string of ponies is magnificent."

Lettice fixed her granddaughter with what was known in the family as the "regal" eye.

"Bull," Lettice said, rapping the table with her hand. The discarded luncheon china and crystal rattled in response. "And who sighed when he rode past? A totally feminine sigh that had nothing to do with horses, I might add."

Anne cursed under her breath at her grandmother's acute hearing. She glared back in defiance and lied. "How would I know?"

"Well, it wasn't me," Lettice said. "And it certainly wasn't Philip."

Anne turned around and looked at her nine-year-old son, perched on the back end of her Jeep, parked behind them. His small body was tense and still as he watched the game. Clearly, he was enraptured.

"Are you sure it was a female sigh?" Anne asked, grinning.

Lettice glanced at the boy, then smiled reluctantly. "Yes, I'm sure, but I won't argue the point."

"For once," Anne muttered.

"I doubt you'll admit to it anyway," Lettice added. "I do wish, though, you hadn't been so stubborn about marrying James."

Anne jerked at the sound of her deepest thoughts coming blithely from her grandmother's lips. So much for a change of subject. She was determined to hold her patience with Lettice, however. The game was almost over, and she could go home to the safety of Makefield Meadows, her stud farm outside Washington's Crossing, released finally from this torture. Still, she couldn't allow Lettice to harbor such a dangerous notion.

"Grandmother, there was nothing to be stubborn about—"

"You two were a perfect match," Lettice went on, oblivious. "I've always thought so. I have never understood why you just couldn't give things a chance."

"Help me, Lord," Anne murmured. A "perfect match" was the last thing she and James would ever be. She'd had one disastrous match with a Hollywood producer who had also owned horses. After that experience she wasn't about to go for two. Besides, James had made his feelings for her all too clear many years ago.

She shrugged again, trying to seem uninterested. "Since our families are friendly, I'm sure you all thought it would have been nice. But I'm not very . . . conventional, Grandmother. Or acceptable. You know that."

"Ridiculous," Lettice said. "You're a Kitteridge."

Anne smiled at her grandmother's pronouncement. As a child she'd overheard too many catty comments about her father marrying his secretary not to know differently. Being a Kitteridge hadn't made her mother "acceptable." Fortunately, her parents hadn't cared. They just went happily along continuing to publish *The World*, her father's travel magazine. Unfortunately, their daughter had always felt a little like an outcast.

"Still," Lettice continued, obviously finding an opening, "why you ever insisted on becoming a professional jockey, or marrying that bas—"

"Grandmother," Anne warned, glancing at Philip. Although she thoroughly agreed with her grandmother's opinion of her ex-husband, Ellis Crawford, she didn't want it said in front of her son. Philip's hearing aid picked up more than people thought. But she needn't have worried. Philip was in pololand.

"Well, now you breed horses," Lettice said, changing gears slightly. "Unfortunately, you won't do it from a desk as others do."

"It's no fun that way," Anne said, grinning. She sobered and added, "It took me a long time to accept that I'll never fit in with this." She waved a hand at the picnickers enjoying the Sport of Princes. "I'll never be Ellen. She was born with the silver spoon. I wasn't. I like who I am, and I like what I do. I'm sorry if that disappoints you, Grandmother."

Lettice harrumphed. "You have never disappointed me, child. It's just that you seem to be deliberately eccentric. But you are more like Ellen than you know. . . ."

Anne laughed. Her cousin was beautiful, always poised and elegant. She had no illusions about herself, however.

"But you're steering me away from the meat of the matter." Lettice raised her eyebrows. "So, my girl, you've never considered marrying James because you think you're unsuitable."

"Grandmother!" Anne exclaimed at the outrageous notion. "That's not at all why—"

"Then if you do think you're suitable, why haven't you gone after him?" Lettice demanded.

"Why should I—" Anne clamped her lips shut. This conversation was losing all semblance of reality. "Grandmother, James and I have never 'clicked,' okay? I threw up on him at my christening. That set the tone of our 'relationship' ever since. Haven't you noticed we rarely see each other as adults? I have too many reasons not to get involved with anyone. And James . . . Well, anything else is just wishful thinking on your part."

The game ended just then, and the cheers of the crowd drew their attention. The score showed that James's team had won. It figured, Anne thought. James, like her cousin, Ellen, fit in effortlessly.

"Mr. Farraday's really good," Philip exclaimed, finally coming out of his trance.

So even her son was enamored . . . and right. She smiled at Philip. "You liked the game."

"It was great. Mom, can I go look at the horses?"

She hesitated for an instant, then nodded. The makeshift stables were about one hundred yards behind the game field. "Be back here in twenty minutes. The stable's a temporary setup, so be careful."

Philip snorted. "I know how to be around a stable, Mom."

She made a face. "So you do. I'm just being a mom."

Philip scrambled out of the Jeep and disappeared into the crowd. Anne suppressed a ripple of anxiety for her son. Near deafness in one ear was hardly cause for maternal overprotectiveness, and she knew it. But she had never quite rid herself of that twinge of worry.

"It's good that you don't fuss over him," Lettice said. "But he's a quiet boy. Sometimes too quiet, I think."

"I know. He needs more confidence." She was trying hard to encourage that in Philip. It was one of the reasons she had let him go just now. California had done its damage. She only hoped it wasn't irreparable.

On the field, the players shook hands with one another, then turned their tired horses toward the stables. Anne had settled back in her lawn chair as they rode past, but Lettice stood up and waved. To Anne's horror, she called out, "James! Stop a moment and have some victory champagne!"

"What the hell are you doing, Grandmother?" Anne whispered fiercely as James turned around.

He waved back and swerved his horse in their direction.

Lettice's look was the soul of innocence. "Being social, dear."

"And I'm Whitney Houston," Anne muttered. She curled her fingers around the polished wood armrests, knowing she couldn't walk away without looking snobbish or silly. Heat flamed her face as she remembered the desire flooding through her body when she had watched him play. Lettice deserved to be roasted over a fire, she decided. James had certainly sparked one in her.

He dismounted and caught her staring before she could turn away. His gaze seemed to bore into her. Dirt streaked his face, but the smile he gave her was almost dazzling in its intimacy. He held the reins of his horse loosely in one hand, the bay following him like an obedient puppy.

The deep throbbing she had finally suppressed surged back hotter and fiercer than before. She desperately wanted to run. Obviously, she was more of a sucker for a man on a horse than she'd thought.

Somehow, she managed to stand as he reached them. She was immediately aware of the mingled scents of man and animal, primitive and enticing. He greeted her grandmother with a kiss on the cheek. Anne immediately stuck out her hand. She doubted he would give her the same greeting, but she wasn't taking any chances.

It was still a mistake.

His fingers reached out and curved around hers . . . and held. She was frozen to the spot, the buzzing in her ears deafening all other sounds. She could feel only his palm pressed hotly to hers, sending signals of ageless sensuality throughout her body. It was as if time were standing still.

James Farraday stared at the woman before him. She was small-boned and slender and more beautiful than ever. A cloud of dark, shoulder-length hair spun around her face like an ethereal halo. Her large blue-green eyes, the Kitteridge trademark, were wide and fathomless. Her slim nose had a slight bump that intrigued rather than marred. Her lips were full and bow-shaped, urging a man to trace them with his finger, his lips, his tongue. Her dress was belted at a waist most women would kill to have, and the yellow linen skimmed over her breasts, hips, and thighs, outlining a body beautifully formed from a lifetime of riding. A simple gold chain necklace and button earrings were her only jewelry.

Annie Kitteridge had bedeviled him from the moment he had seen her as a baby, and she bedeviled him now more than ever. She had always been independent and stubborn, and possessed a vitality that shone out of her. He was glad it hadn't been dimmed by a bad marriage. The thought of that marriage made his hackles rise. He wasn't sure who or what to hate for it. He just knew a cruel twist of fate had shown him once what could be with Anne . . . and then denied her to him.

He ached now to touch more than her hand; he wanted to explore her hidden secrets. It didn't matter that they were in a field full of people. He would give anything to know if her mouth still held that sweet fire that had haunted his dreams for so long. But he could sense new barriers erected around her, barriers he was tempted to challenge. He knew he would never allow himself the pleasure. He had good reason not to.

Still, he had been hoping she'd be here today. After the telephone call he had received this morning, he had a proposition for her. Quite a proposition.

"Your champagne, James."

Lettice's voice broke the spell with a painful snap. As James let go of her hand, Anne could hear a mental clock re-starting somewhere inside her. She pulled herself up and straightened her shoulders.

"It's nice to see you again, James," she said in a polite tone. "Congratulations on the game."

James grinned as he took the filled champagne glass from Lettice. "I feel as if I've been through a war. You look beautiful, Anne. I'm glad you came."

She smiled her reply, not trusting her voice.

"I hope it will *not* take me months of pleading to get you to come to another game, Anne," Lettice said to her. "Especially as you can see how much Philip enjoys it." She added for James's benefit, "He's at the stables now. Probably looking at your horses."

"I hope he likes them."

"He probably will," Anne muttered.

"I wonder if it's a faux pas to play all out against royalty to win," Lettice speculated aloud.

"I'm sure Prince Charles wouldn't have it any other way, Grandmother," Anne said, grateful for the idle conversation. That fire was still licking through her, and she needed to regain her composure.

"Our friend from England is a real fighter." James chuckled. "He enjoyed himself out there."

"It was very gracious of him to play while he's here on an official visit."

Anne choked back her laughter, knowing Lettice had arranged the match to entice the royal visitor and thereby gain prestige and needed money for one of her charities. "I don't think he stood a chance."

"I know he didn't," James said, grinning at Lettice. He turned back to Anne. "Annie, I need to talk to you—"

He was interrupted by several women suddenly flocking around him. He gave all of them a charming smile, and an odd pain knifed through Anne. She judged the other women were in their early thirties. She didn't recognize any of them, but she'd bet her trust fund there was a Muffy, Buffy, or Babs in the group. There always was. Worse, the women were beautiful, very feminine in their flowered silk dresses and floppy hats. Her own dress now seemed too tailored and out of place. And the way they fluttered around James made her think of hot-house flowers desperate for a little pollenation. They probably were.

The interruption was for the best, she decided. She didn't know which was worse. James needing to talk to her . . . or him calling her by her childhood nickname.

James's horse, startled by the sudden influx of strange humans, whinnied his dismay and pulled free of his master's loose grip. A scared horse was a potentially dangerous one, Anne knew. Sure enough, before anyone could grab his reins, the horse wreaked his own brand of havoc.

He walked over to Anne, butted his nose against her chest, and blew gustily down the front of her dress in a horsey sign of affection.

Anne pushed the horse's head away in one deft movement, then gazed at her now ruined dress. She sighed in resignation.

James got the women. She got the horse. Dudley Do-right would have been proud of her.

"The last animal who did this to me, bub," she said to the horse, "got curried with a brush that had five-inch steel bristles."

The horse butted her chest again.

"Masochist," she muttered, giving in and scratching the animal on its long black muzzle.

Under her hand, the animal's hide was soaked in sweat. She set her jaw in anger as she felt the rest of the horse's head and neck. While James was drinking champagne and flirting with his "flowers," his horse had been left to sweat in exhaustion. A good horseman took care of his animal before himself. At least the horse wasn't lathered, but it still needed to be cooled down and taken to the stables. She was ashamed that she had been so preoccupied with James, she hadn't noticed the animal's plight before this.

"I'm sorry, Anne," James said, breaking away from his groupies. He patted the horse on the neck. "Monroe does that when he likes someone."

"So I discovered."

James grinned. "He has excellent taste. But your dress. . . . Get a new one and send me the bill."

"That's very nice of you," she said while privately deciding she'd be damned before she did. She handed over the reins. "He needs attention, James."

"I know." He looked around the field. "The groom should have come for him by now. But I figured this might happen. That's why I can spare only a minute. You'll be at the dance tonight, right?"

"I don't think so," she said, ruthlessly forcing away a flush of embarrassment. She knew she shouldn't feel embarrassed that she'd pointed out his horse needed attention.

"Yes, she is going," Lettice corrected her.

Anne glared at her grandmother. She had forgotten about the damn dance tonight. She couldn't go now. "I know I agreed to come to the match,

Grandmother, but I shouldn't be away from the farm at this time of year—"

"Nonsense." Lettice glared right back. "You have very competent people working for you. They know you are only a phone call away. Besides, you wouldn't want to disappoint me, would you? Or James."

Anne gritted her teeth, knowing she was caught in a social trap. "Of course not."

"Good," James said. "I'll see you there. It's important." He stared at her for a moment longer, then gulped back the last of his champagne and shoved the glass into her hands. He turned to Lettice. "I'll take Monroe to the stables, then come back for the trophy presentation. They'll want you at that too, Lettice. After all, you arranged this match."

"I'll go with you to the stables," one of the other women volunteered.

"Thanks, Buffy," James said, "but it's hectic back there. And very dirty. I wouldn't want you to ruin that beautiful dress."

Buffy looked both shocked and grateful, and Anne hid a smile. She had made a sure bet with her trust fund. Buffy did look . . . enchanting. Anne forced away the urge to shred the Gibson Girl hat the woman was wearing. It was a silly thought. Anyway, Lettice would kill her if she did.

It was then she realized all of the women were scowling at her as if she had deliberately forced the horse to ruin her dress and draw James's attention from them. She arched her eyebrows and gazed at them in cool defiance.

James took the horse to the stables, Buffy and crew electing to forgo that pleasure.

"So much for your ideas about James, Grandmother," Anne said in a low voice as the other women departed.

"Nonsense. A little competition is good for the soul," Lettice said. "James is an attractive boy. You certainly wouldn't want someone who scratches himself every ten seconds, now, would you?"

Anne eyed the other women sourly as they teetered away, their ridiculously high heels sinking into the ground. She also admitted her grandmother might have a point.

"No comment," she finally said.

"Naturally, you wouldn't," Lettice said. "I better get over to the presentation. Then we'll go home and change for the dance."

As her grandmother headed for the knot of officials on the playing field, Anne shook her head and began to pack up the remains of their picnic.

"There is no way I will be at that damn dance tonight," she muttered to herself. After her gaping schoolgirl reaction to James, she'd be stupid to expose herself again to his charm.

Incredibly stupid.

Two

Okay, so she was incredibly stupid.

Anne grimaced as she watched the elegantly dressed men and women swirl around the dance floor. She stood almost directly behind a potted palm in the archway, as good a spot as any while she waited for her grandmother to finish "fussing" in the ladies' room.

She had tried to get out of the dance yet again, but arguing with her grandmother was like trying to stop a race horse from running. A useless gesture but one that sometimes had to be made. Lettice had promised, however, that she would never ask her to one of these things again—if she came tonight. Although Anne had her misgivings about this particular evening, it was a bargain she couldn't pass up.

Pulling at her gown's bodice, she cursed herself yet again for not looking in her closet earlier. The gown she was wearing was a leftover from her California days. All her evening wear was. It had seemed so tame then. But it could be worse, she thought. She could have worn the red.

She spotted her cousin, Ellen Kitteridge-Carlini, on the dance floor with her new husband, Joe. Ellen had suffered through a bad marriage and the loss of a child. It was good to see her so radiant and happy now. Anne frowned. It was funny, but she'd always thought James and Ellen would have been perfect together. Yet seeing Ellen with Joe only proved how wrong her original perception was.

She leaned back against the wall and closed her eyes. She hadn't seen James—yet. Maybe he wasn't here tonight. Her reaction to him that afternoon had haunted her for the rest of the day. She had finally concluded that it had been seeing him with horses. What else could explain her gaping at him like a dizzy kid? She'd done that once before. Once was enough.

Tonight she would be cool and calm. She'd put on a cloak of sophistication. She only hoped she had one somewhere.

"Annie."

At the sound of a deep, all too familiar voice, Anne jumped . . . right into the palm tree. She grabbed for it as it started to tip over, the sharp fronds whipping around her in a frenzied attack. The palm came completely away from its heavy pot, the dirt surrounding the roots as dry as a desert. Hugging the tree to her, she focused her gaze on James.

"Hello," she said brightly as she set the palm back into the pot as casually as possible. First his horse picked her dress to snort all over, and now this, she thought. She'd be lucky if she didn't fall into the champagne fountain tonight.

She turned around and matters were made worse by the sight of him in evening wear. His tuxedo fit like the proverbial glove, and she tried desperately not to stare. She was all too aware that she was virtually alone with James . . . and the palm tree. She couldn't think of a better place to be—except prison, maybe.

"Hello," he said. "I'm glad I found you—"

It took James several seconds to realize his greeting had stopped abruptly when she turned around. It took him several more to realize he was staring at her. Her ankle-length gown in shimmering turquoise crepe clung to her every curve. The sleeves and torso glittered with blue and silver bangles, and the skirt glimmered with woven silver threads. Any jewelry, other than earrings, would have been gaudy. But it was the keyhole opening from throat to below her breasts that captured his attention. Her cleavage was completely exposed. The bodice was incredibly daring, and he wondered at the engineering feat that kept it in place. One slip and more than cleavage would see the light of day. He tried to shift his gaze from the sight of her creamy flesh, but it was impossible. The temptation to find out if her skin was as silken as it looked was nearly overwhelming.

"I think I forgive you for throwing up on me when I was four," he finally said, grinning at her.

"Very funny." Her cheeks looked flushed. "It's nice to see you too, James."

"Not as nice as it is to . . . see you." His grin widened. "That's a beautiful dress. But don't you feel a little chilly?"

"Trust me, this is tame next to something Cher would wear," she replied, fixing him with a fair imitation of her grandmother's stare. "Anyway, I've seen more daring ones here tonight."

That might be, he conceded, but none affected him as hers did. She was not like those women who had fluttered around him after the polo match that afternoon. Not at all. He didn't like the thought that other men had seen her in that gown. But he had no rights to her. He'd given up that privilege on a long-ago summer night. . . .

He reminded himself that he hadn't had a chance to speak to her earlier about his business proposition, and that was the only right he could have to her. After the phone call he'd received this morning, he knew he had an offer she couldn't refuse—and one he couldn't imagine sharing with anyone but her. Only she would understand and appreciate the momentous thing he had done.

Forcing himself to ignore the distractions she presented, he asked, "Can I ask why you're hiding behind the palm?"

"Waiting for Grandmother," she said.

"I see. Then I'll wait with you. We have to talk, Annie. Privately—"

"Anne," she corrected him firmly. "It's just Anne now."

He smiled. "You have never been 'just Anne.' "

Before she could protest, he joined her at the wall, leaning his shoulder against the flocked paper and effectively trapping her between him and the palm. He was immediately aware of the small space separating them. His body and mind urged him closer, to take her in his arms and inhale the scent of light perfume and woman, feel her curves under his hands.

He set his jaw to keep himself in control. He had a business arrangement for her, that was all.

He looked around the ballroom and knew they could be interrupted at any moment. He would have to get her alone. He ignored the leap of his senses at the thought, and said, "I do have to talk to you privately, but this isn't nearly private enough. There are some rooms along the back hallway—"

"I really hate to disappoint you, James, but I promised Grandmother I would wait for her. She'd be upset if I weren't here."

He stared at her in disbelief. "Are we talking about the same Lettice Kitteridge?"

"Yes. And when she expects you to be somewhere, you'd better be there."

He acknowledged she did know her Lettice. "Fine, then we'll wait."

A few minutes later she looked a little too relieved when Lettice finally emerged from the ladies' room. She hurried toward her grandmother.

"Anne, hold it!" he exclaimed, following her.

"Thank you for waiting with me," she said over her shoulder, "but I have to go now—"

"Anne!"

"I see you found James," Lettice said when they both reached her.

"I didn't know I was lost," he said.

Lettice chuckled.

"The family's waiting, Grandmother," Anne said. "Besides, James probably brought someone with him tonight."

He frowned. "I did bring my mother . . . oh, you mean a date. No, actually, I didn't."

"Then you can join us for a while," Lettice said. "Some of my brood are here, but you know them all."

"Thank you, Lettice," he said, noting Anne's

blank expression. He wondered at it, then added, "May I borrow Anne? I need to talk with her privately. We won't be long, I promise."

"Ahh . . ." Anne began.

"Of course you can," Lettice said, smiling in clear pleasure. Most people found her dictatorial, but he cared for her as if she were a second grandmother.

"Thanks. You're terrific."

"But . . . but . . ." Anne stuttered as he took her arm and led her away.

"Enjoy yourselves," Lettice called after them.

"Where are you taking me?" she asked, hurrying to keep up with him."

"Someplace very private."

Anne instantly dug in her heels and stopped. James spun around.

"Dammit, Anne. What are you doing?"

"The question is, what are *you* doing?" she demanded. "What is all this about?"

He glanced around the corridor. "Not here."

"Yes—"

She never got any farther. James marched her over to the nearest door, opened it, and thrust her into a small sitting room. He joined her, closing the door behind them.

No one else was in the room. The blood surged in his veins at the notion.

"James, what are—"

"Ever hear of a horse named Battle Cry?" he interrupted. He'd waited all day to tell her. He wasn't waiting a moment longer.

"Who hasn't?" she said in an angry voice. "Descendant of Man o'War and last year's Triple Crown winner. He's the hottest and most talked about horse since his ancestor. But what does that have to do with anything?"

James grinned in excitement. He couldn't wait to see her face. "It has everything to do with anything, Annie my girl. I bought him this morning."

Anne gasped in astonishment. Her ears had to be deceiving her.

"It took me months to arrange this," he went on. "The sale finally went through this morning. All I have to do is sign the papers."

"But . . . but . . ."

"I'm retiring him from racing as of today and putting him out to stud." He reached out and tightly gripped her arms. "What do you think of having him at your farm?"

The room spun wildly. Hot shivers ran down her back, and her lungs couldn't seem to get enough air. She wasn't sure that it was the idea of Battle Cry procreating future winners at her farm . . . or James's touch.

She stepped away from him and back against the wall in an attempt to regain her composure. She also needed to put some distance between them. Shock and an odd disappointment ran through her. She didn't know what she'd been expecting when James had insisted on speaking privately to her, but this certainly wasn't it.

Battle Cry, she thought. Some said he was a reincarnation of Man o'War, the most famous racing horse ever. Man o'War had lost only one race in his career, Battle Cry only two. And James wanted to entrust the horse to her. She had worked hard to bring top quality stallions and mares to her farm, and she'd just started having some success. James must have heard about her efforts. But Battle Cry was already the horse of the decade. If his progeny carried on the tradition, he'd be the horse of the century. It was too good to be true.

"Annie. You look as if you're going to faint."

His voice was filled with amusement. She opened her eyes.

"I *do* feel as if I might faint," she said. She took a deep breath and straightened from the wall.

"Will you do it?"

He was so handsome, she thought. A sensual magnetism radiated from him, continually pulling at its female counterpart in her. Her reaction to him was growing, and it scared her. She knew she would have to have contact with him as the owner of Battle Cry. The notion was daunting. She could handle it, she sternly told herself. It wouldn't be as bad as she thought. The most conscientious owners checked on their horses only every few months, and called in between. *None* came every week, or even every month. Thank goodness. She'd be idiotic not to take Battle Cry just because she was attracted to his owner.

James was grinning like a kid with a new Nintendo. She grinned in return. It was infectious.

"I was just thinking that I'd be crazy not to take the horse." She hesitated, then steeled herself to ask a basic question. "Have you had him tested yet for . . . potency?"

"He's got what it takes." She blushed, then he dropped another devastating bomb. "I know I should have approached you before this, but I wanted to keep the negotiations quiet. If it got out that he was being sold instead of racing this year as he was supposed to, I would have had way too many competitors for him. There were a couple of shrewd investors I had to outbid as it was.

The news would have leaked out if I had talked with one of the big stud farms in Kentucky or California about placing him. Anyway, I thought of you instantly."

She struggled against a wave of anger and humiliation. He wanted to place the horse with her to momentarily hide the sale. After the papers were signed, sealed, and delivered, she had a pretty good idea what would happen. He would move Battle Cry to a more prestigious farm. In her own excitement she had forgotten that it was March, halfway through this year's breeding season. All the top mares would already be committed for the year. If she had been thinking straight, she might have remembered . . . and wondered.

She was about to open her mouth and tell him exactly where he could take his million-dollar-horse factory, when she remembered her own mare, Lollipop's Rainbow, hadn't "taken" in her last mating. She would come into season again in a few weeks—just about the time Battle Cry would arrive. Provided she agreed to take him.

She shouldn't, she thought. It wasn't . . . right.

"Don't worry, James. My lips are sealed," she said, deciding she was entitled to a little something for allowing her farm to be a horse hideout. And Battle Cry had to hide out somewhere.

"Good," he said, yet he sounded oddly distracted.

She knew she should be asking more questions, but James was staring at her mouth. The room suddenly seemed hot and airless, and disturbingly intimate. Anne swallowed, the space separating them growing even smaller, though neither of them had moved. Her body was frozen to the spot as a shocking awareness surged through her bloodstream. She wondered if humans went through a mating season, when logic and sanity were lost to potent natural drives. She had no desire to get involved with a man—and James was completely wrong for so many reasons. And yet here she was, wanting him to touch her, wanting to touch him in return.

He seemed to lean forward . . . then stepped away.

"Come on," he said, reaching for the doorknob and opening the door. "Your grandmother is probably wondering what happened to us."

The heat inside her was replaced by the chill of rejection. She knew she ought to feel grateful that he wasn't interested. Anyway, he had his groupies and she certainly didn't care to number among them.

She lifted her chin and said, "You're right. Better not say anything to Grandmother about the horse just yet though. She's got a communications system that works faster than fiber optics."

He chuckled. "You forget. I see it in action with my own grandmother. Believe me, ITT would pay a fortune to have it."

He escorted her through the door and back into the corridor. Her muscles, more tense than she'd thought, relaxed when she saw the other guests. She decided she deserved an award for not making a fool of herself. The potential for it had been frightening.

As they walked together, he took her elbow in a gesture of good manners. She decided she wasn't out of the woods yet as a sensual heat flowed into her at the slight touch of his fingers.

"This is probably a moot point," he finally said, "but I should see your place, shouldn't I? I'd like to do it as soon as possible, so we can ship the horse."

He didn't have to rub it in, she thought murderously. He might be sexy as hell, but he had a lot to learn about her. She forced herself to smile. "Most owners like to know what the facilities are."

He smiled too, and in spite of her anger her heart flipped over. "Yours, I've heard, are fine. Battle Cry's owners were concerned about his future home. When I told them I had you in mind, they were pleased with the choice."

They reached the Kitteridge table before she could reply, though his remark pleased her . . . and puzzled her. Several family members were at the table. About the only one missing was her cousin, Susan, who was very active in the Washington, D.C. Party Circuit. Ann wished she were with Susan right now. Lettice's eyes were gleaming in clear anticipation.

Anne sat down next to her grandmother, taking her time settling herself into the seat.

"Drink?" James asked, laughter underlying his tone.

"Thank you," she said primly. She almost liked him for playing along. "A tonic, please."

"Lettice?"

"I'm fine," the older woman nearly snapped.

Anne hid her smile. Clearly, Lettice wanted to pump her privately.

James headed for the bar. The moment he was out of earshot, her grandmother rounded on her.

"Well?" she asked. "What were you two talking about?"

"Yes," Ellen added, leaning forward. "I'm a little curious, too, about what you were doing with James. I thought you didn't like him."

"Honestly," Anne muttered, then decided to play a bold card. "Relax, everyone. We were only talking about one of his horses. No big deal."

The others nodded and turned back to their earlier conversation. No one would think twice about her and James talking horses. After all, she raised them, and he rode them. A calculated risk, but a small one with this crowd.

However, her grandmother eyed her thoughtfully. Anne sensed Lettice could feel the truth of her words—yet she wasn't quite buying it. Still, the truth—when it finally surfaced—would squelch any notions her grandmother might be having now.

Anne allowed herself a smile, thinking of her plans for Lollipop's Rainbow. Before this was over, James would be in for a few surprises too.

Three

He watched the horse gallop along the path of the quarter-mile drive. The morning mist couldn't hide the rider snug on the animal's back. Even though his car was behind them on the drive, he could easily discern Anne's dark hair tangling with the horse's mane as she rode high on its shoulders.

Dammit, James thought, as she and the horse literally flew across the ground. She should look helpless, but she didn't. He knew that as a professional jockey, she had ridden all kinds of horses in all kinds of situations. Her mastery over this animal was obvious. And the other night she had been incredible in that dress. Her combination of femininity and steel was intoxicating.

He wondered now if placing Battle Cry here was as wise a decision as he'd originally thought. As a child, he'd seen Anne only when he'd been dragged to the Kitteridges' on social visits during holidays and summer vacations from military school. He'd been relieved when she left for California soon after that night he'd kissed her. Since she'd been back, he'd avoided her. A man with secrets could offer nothing to a woman. He'd been all too abruptly reminded of that earlier time when he had misread the highway numbers and nearly gone the wrong way. He wouldn't forget again.

A dull pain lanced through him at the thought.

He noticed she had stopped the horse by a white-painted fence to feed carrots to the mares and foals there. He stopped the car and rolled down the window. Chilly air infiltrated the heat inside the Jaguar.

"Wanna race?" he asked.

She laughed, her eyes sparkling. "Don't tempt me. Digby likes to run, but he's done enough already. He needs to cool down."

"I'd probably lose anyway," James admitted, eyeing the prancing horse. Although the animal was wet with perspiration from the hard ride, its healthy, rippling muscles announced all too clearly Digby's desire to take on anything—even a car.

Anne grinned at him, then sobered abruptly, as if a switch had been thrown. He had no idea what could have caused her to change so quickly. Her tone was matter-of-fact as she said, "Go on up the drive. You can park in front of the house and walk around to the right. The main stables are there. I'll follow you in."

He did as she suggested, glancing frequently in the rearview mirror. She was following more slowly, visually checking fences. He had noticed horses and foals in the fields on both sides of the drive, and it reassured him to see her keeping an eye on her charges.

By the time he reached the house, he knew his glances in the mirror had been more than curiosity. Something inside him had insisted on just looking at her. In the past few days he'd been drawn to her more and more, and he hadn't expected that. He'd have to try even harder to control it.

He pulled the car into the semi-circular drive in front of her house. It was an old Federal brick two-story with a white-columned portico, and though small in size, it was warm and cozy-looking. His condominium building was sterile and cold by comparison.

He had no sooner parked the car and stepped out, when a dog that looked like a half-sized Doberman pinscher walked over and sat down in front of him. Its teeth, however, would have matched its bigger cousins any day. Although the dog had bared its teeth only for a moment, it was very clear to James that he would not be allowed to move away from his car.

"Great," he muttered, staring back at the dog. He had the feeling his leg, if not the rest of him, was being considered as breakfast.

Anne's horse cantered down the last of the long dirt drive. The dog turned and looked at her, then turned back to James. The hair on its neck bristled, and it crouched low, growling deep in its throat, ready to spring.

"Tibbs!" Anne called. "He's okay."

Tibbs growled once more, then sat back on his haunches.

"A minute ago you were content just to look at me," James said to the dog.

Anne laughed. "He's a Manchester terrier, and he likes to show me how tough he is. He thinks he'll get an extra treat if he does."

"I think he ought to get two."

The front door burst open, drawing their attention. Philip raced over the threshold like a Kentucky Derby winner.

"Hi, Mom! I'm trying not to be late for the bus. Come on, Tibbs, race ya. Hi, Mr. Farraday!"

Boy and dog were off instantly down the drive.

"Good morning, Philip. It's nice to see you too," Anne said to her son's rapidly disappearing back.

James chuckled.

"Kids are wonderful," she said dryly as she got off her horse.

She dismounted in smooth, sure movements, and the blood began to pound through his veins at the sight she presented. Her jeans were faded and soft, and the damn things clung to her legs as if molded to them. His temperature rose alarmingly as he stared at her. He remembered how she had suddenly blossomed at seventeen, her teenage gawkiness turning to slender grace. It was an image he didn't allow himself to remember. Until now.

"I didn't think you would show up," she said, motioning for him to join her as she walked the horse the rest of the way in. "Not for morning rounds, at least."

"I told you on the phone I would," he said, frowning in puzzlement. She had given him the choice of early morning or late afternoon to visit her farm. "Why would you think I wouldn't come now?"

She shrugged. "You don't strike me as a morning person."

He grinned. "I'd surprise you."

"Let's take the fifty-cent tour," she said, clearly ignoring his remark.

His grin widened at her deliberate change of

subject. He was tempted to keep up the sexy teasing, but he let it go for the moment. He didn't know how far he could go without getting into trouble. Anne was too tempting.

"What prompted you to buy a race horse?" she asked, leading the way around the house to the stables. "You're not obligated to answer, but I thought your interest was with the polo ponies."

"I make investments," he said. "I'm a venture capitalist. I've done pretty well so far for my clients, but this is my first venture with a race horse."

"I—" She looked away as if embarrassed. "I didn't know you worked . . . I mean, had a profession."

"You do, so why shouldn't I?" he asked, chuckling. "Anyway, I can't play polo all day."

She laughed. "Okay, so we're both eccentric. Battle Cry is an investment for you, then."

"Yes."

"People do like horses for that reason."

He frowned at her cool tone. Now that he was physically closer to her, he could sense hostility in her. He also sensed it was directed at him, and he had no idea why. Tibbs had nothing on his mistress for a sudden change of mood.

Before he could ask what was wrong, he saw the cinder path had led them to several long, low buildings. Each set of stables was U-shaped around a center courtyard, and each was immaculately maintained. "This one," Anne said, pointing, "and the building behind it are the mares' stables. Right now we're about two-thirds full. The breeding season is in the spring, and most of the mares here now will go back home after it's over. Some are boarded here year-round."

"I understand mares come to the stallions, not

the other way around," James said, watching several grooms bustle around various individual horse boxes.

"Right. The mares come into . . . 'season' right after they give birth, so they have their foals here. By the time the breeding season's over, the foals are strong enough to travel, and hopefully, the mares will be in foal again."

"Digby must love it," James said, patting her horse's neck. The horse's ears flicked, but he accepted the strange touch.

Anne laughed. "Actually, Digby couldn't care less. He's a gelding. I bought him when he was being retired from racing at age ten. Geldings have a longer racing life than colts, which go out to stud."

James patted the animal again, this time in commiseration. "You have no idea what you're missing, Digby."

"Well, don't tell him," Anne said, flipping the reins through an iron ring on one of the hitching posts. She stopped one of the grooms. "Rob, will you take care of Digby, please? We have a customer."

The groom nodded, then led the horse away.

As they continued the tour, James saw the buildings were set in a wide semi-circle separated from one another by large paddocks. A neat cinder path led between the paddocks to each building. After the mares' stables came a smaller one called the foaling stable, where the births actually took place. Several mares were in various stages of labor, and Anne consulted with Jonas, the gray-haired man in charge, who assured her all was going well. James gazed at the mares as he waited, fascinated by the thought of new life about to emerge into the world. He was grateful for the break in breeding conversation. Talking about sex of any kind with Anne was giving him notions he couldn't pursue.

The dog rejoined them when they left the foaling stable, and to James's amusement completely ignored him. Their next stop was a large barn that housed the stallions. James admitted that the three currently there were impressive.

"Michael's Harp, A Bit of Blarney, and Redman Chief," Anne said, pointing to each one in turn. "Or, as they're known around here: Jim, Bob, and Ned. The fancy names are for the racing forms. Redman's mine, and the other two are boarded here. The first foals out of them have started racing now as two-year-olds. And winning. I have plenty of room for Battle Cry . . . for as long as you plan to keep him here."

James nodded. He could easily envision Battle Cry joining these three, and the image was very satisfying. What wasn't satisfying, however, was Anne's businesslike manner during this tour. She had kept a noticeable space between them the entire time. At least he noticed it. And she held herself tensely, as if angry with him. It could be her way of establishing a business relationship with him, but that didn't mean he had to like it.

Once outside the stallion barn, she said, "That's about it."

"What's that building there?" he asked, pointing to another barn farther along the path. It was the last building on the curve.

She was silent for a long moment. "Breeding shed."

"Can I see it?" he asked, curious about the building.

It took her an even longer time to answer, and

he wondered why she was hesitating. He could understand if it were in use, but the place looked deserted.

"All right," she finally said. "Nothing's scheduled this early in the day. But it's just like a regular barn, really."

They walked over, and she unlocked a man-door in the huge roll-aside entrance. Inside, the building was quiet, even their own footsteps hushed by the thick covering of straw on the floor.

James thought of what took place there, and knew why she had hesitated to put it on the tour. The ordinary-looking walls seemed to reverberate with the sounds and images of countless animals responding in magnificent passion to nature's ageless demand for procreation.

His own senses heightened with awareness of the woman next to him. Pictures of her raced through his mind in a kaleidoscope of his deepest fantasies. His blood heated and throbbed.

Anne felt as if her lungs were suddenly empty of breath and knew she had to put space between them. She moved farther into the barn and leaned against the door of the building's only stall, wishing yet again she could have ended the tour gracefully at the stallion barn.

"How many places do you plan to sell for Battle Cry during the season?" she asked, her voice sounding faint.

James took a deep breath to regain control of his surging body. "I understand forty mares are the average a stallion can . . . accommodate during the breeding season. I thought I would offer forty places."

"About forty is average. Some do less and get exhausted. Some can handle more." She could feel heat creeping into her face at her words. She'd had this conversation with many other horse owners and never once flinched. Why was it so difficult with this one?

"Lucky horse," he murmured. The urge to close the space between them and take her into his arms was pounding through him. Instead, he pivoted and stared out the open door. She cleared her throat, and he turned back.

"It all depends on the horse," she said. "They act on instinct, and . . . nature knows how to press that button—"

Anne instantly stopped. Her own instincts were raging, as if every one of her buttons had been pressed. Her body was hot and tight with the desire to throw herself into his arms and go wherever nature took them. She wanted to know again that unique fit of his mouth on hers, the complete havoc his kiss could wreak on her senses. She wanted it again and hated herself for it.

James didn't move. He knew he would pull her to him if he did. He wanted her, right here, right now, in this place where nature was at its most primitive and most grand. If he touched her, he wouldn't be able to stop. How, he wondered dimly, could she be so damn nonchalant about the conversation while he was being driven insane?

"Still," she went on, "horses aren't machines, and Thoroughbreds are especially high-strung and sometimes fussier than other breeds." Anne wanted to run. Her attempt to distract herself with conversation was only making things worse. She somehow had to lighten the subject. The consequences didn't bear thinking about if she couldn't. "Thoroughbreds are notorious for needing 'companions' —other horses, mules, even cats, dogs, or birds— with them at all times or they won't run. When I was riding professionally, there was one horse who wouldn't run unless you squirted it with Shalimar perfume before a race."

The ridiculous story broke the sensual spell, and James laughed, the tension going out of him slowly but steadily. "You're kidding, aren't you?"

His laughter made her relax a little, enough to regain her equilibrium. She shook her head and smiled at him. "No. It's true. And it had to be Shalimar. Nobody knew why it worked, but there was a protest by the other trainers that the perfume was the same as doping the horse, and they wanted the perfume-squirting to stop. Nobody could figure that one out for a ruling. Fortunately, I've never heard that Battle Cry has any quirks."

"Let's hope he doesn't acquire them," he said, wondering if horses could be gay. It was a horrifying thought when he considered how much he'd invested. He joined her at the stall and leaned his elbows on the top rail. There was a space still between them, but it was more comfortable. Even friendly. Almost. Aloud, he added, "Forty mares, then."

"You know you'll charge the mares' owners a fixed fee for the first three years, until his issue start racing. Then the fee shifts up or down depending on whether he's producing winners or not. In England the fee is paid no matter what, but in the United States, if there's no live foal, the fee is refunded. There will probably be several mares a season who don't take or who 'slip.' Miscarry. Life is a fragile thing."

His sanity was a fragile thing, he thought. And being this close to her was enough to drive him over the edge. It nearly had once before, all those years earlier.

"The gestation period for a horse is eleven months," she continued. "Thoroughbreds are officially given a January first birthdate for racing purposes, so the mares need to foal as close to that date as possible. They begin racing as two-year-olds."

He realized that his control was slipping again. The talk was skirting dangerous territory, and it was hazardous being this close to her. Close enough to smell her faint perfume, feel the warmth of her body . . . He straightened away from the rail and said, "So as the owner of the stallion, I can sell a hundred and twenty places, three years' worth, at a fixed price."

"Yes." She was quiet for a long moment. "It is customary to give a place to your breeder. In turn, we waive the boarding fee. I have a mare, Lollipop's Rainbow. Her lines are impeccable—"

He broke in. "I was going to suggest that a place was yours if you wanted. I didn't know it was customary. Do you want any more places? You're more than welcome to them."

"Thank you, but no," she said, shocked and confused by his generous offer. He could charge the earth for a stud fee and get away with it. She felt guilty for trying to sneak Lollipop past him. "I have only the one racing mare. My other tends to produce jumpers."

He nodded. "So if I divide the cost of Battle Cry by one hundred and twenty"—he grinned—"one hundred and nineteen places, and charge that as the individual stud fee, he'll pay back the original investment in three to four years, allowing for the occasional refund of the fee. The horse will have many years of . . . partying ahead of him, all at pure profit for his owner. That makes a horse one of the best investments on earth."

"Only if you get the right one," Anne said.

"Don't depress me."

"I'm sure you'll get your original investment back right on schedule. Before schedule." She moved away from the rail, and whatever easy conversation had been between them was gone. "I'm sorry, James, but the tour's over. I'm afraid I have work to do this morning."

She strode out of the barn, and he stared after her, not sure what had gone wrong. She confused him and bewitched him. He wanted to follow her, but knew it was better this way.

It was Battle Cry going out to stud. Not him.

"Yes, I can accommodate her. . . . Yes, I know her bloodlines are excellent. . . . Yes, it is a wonderful opportunity. . . ."

Anne held her patience as she listened to the man on the other end of the phone positively gush over the prospect of breeding his mare to Battle Cry. She hadn't realized men could gush. The official announcement about Battle Cry retiring to stud had been made only three days earlier, and she had already received twenty phone calls from broodmare owners whose horses were suddenly available. Battle Cry would arrive in a few days, and he'd be busy from the moment he set hoof on the property.

She finally hung up a few minutes later, resisting the temptation to slam the receiver onto the hook. She sat at her paper-strewn desk and uttered every curse word she could think of. James was selling the places to his horse quicker than it had run the Preakness. At this rate Battle Cry would run out of "ammunition" long before the season was through.

She leaned her forehead onto the desktop and groaned at the thought of her conversation with James on the day of the tour. If she had used any more euphemisms for sex, she would have turned into a thesaurus. And she had nearly lost all her control when they'd been alone in the breeding shed.

Her skin went hot as she remembered how desperately she had wanted him to touch her. For some odd reason she felt rejected that he hadn't. She knew it was silly; she knew she ought to be darn grateful nothing had happened. Her marriage had taught her several hard lessons about men. And she'd be foolish if she ever got involved with one of her owners. Some had tried, but she'd easily kept them at a distance. James might be "perfect," but he was a combination of trouble she didn't need.

Yet if she closed her eyes, she could almost feel the strength in his shoulders, the hard muscles of his back. She could feel his chest bare against her breasts, his hands caressing and stroking her. And she could feel her own hands traveling downward, following the line of his ribs, his hard stomach, his hips . . .

"Ahhh!" she cried in a strangled voice, jumping up out of her chair.

She paced around the braided rug covering the

polished plank floor of her study. It was as if she already *had* touched him.

She stopped her pacing. Bracing her hands on the back of her desk chair, she closed her eyes.

She had touched him before. So long ago. It was a memory she never allowed herself to remember. But now she remembered all too well. She had been seventeen and had finally discovered there was more to life than horses. There were boys.

Not boys, she thought, not even one boy. A man. She had had the worst crush on James that summer he'd come home from college. In fact, she'd had it so bad she had cheerfully gone to every social function her grandmother had wanted, just to get a glimpse of him. He had been distant and brooding at first—until the night of that dance. He'd noticed her that night. More than noticed. He had danced with her, and they had been laughing and at ease with each other. And every touch had been magic. There was no other word for the shiver of awareness that had run through her continually at his touch. And then they had gone out onto the balcony.

"I can't believe how much you've changed, Annie," he'd said, taking her hand.

She had smiled, afraid and hungry for him at the same time . . . and he'd pulled her closer. His lips had caressed hers lightly, giving her a chance to pull away.

Anne's face went hot as she remembered how fast she had *not* pulled away. Her arms had wound tightly around his neck, her fingers digging into his shoulders as she'd opened her mouth to him. His tongue had delved in, tasting, teasing, driving her into the first floods of desire. His hands had touched her briefly, but in ways that had left her moaning for more. And her heart . . .

Lord help her, Anne thought, her heart had blossomed like a rose awakening to the first kiss of the sun.

Then the fairy tale had turned into a nightmare. He had pulled away abruptly, leaving her bewildered and hurting. What had she done wrong? She never knew. He never called. In fact, he barely spoke to her again. She left for California a month later to nurse her wounds.

"It was only one damn kiss," she muttered, opening her eyes.

Her sensual response to him in the breeding shed rose to haunt her again, and she groaned. She was more than ready for a second kiss. All her worst fears about working with James were coming true.

The only thing that had saved her in the breeding shed was the way he had talked about Battle Cry, as if the horse were just another blue-chip investment on the stock exchange. She knew people used horses as an investment. But horses had a verve and a gentleness that were unique. It was almost a sacrilege to her to think of horses as an item on a profit and loss statement. To a true horse-person, it was the animal, not the investment, that was important. Clearly, James didn't think that way.

"Damn him," she muttered, telling herself she shouldn't feel guilty for thinking of trying to con a place with Battle Cry for Lollipop's Rainbow. James was about as greedy as they came.

She was committed to Battle Cry, and truthfully, she wanted that horse at her farm. She should take heart in the fact that James was planning on keeping the horse with her for the rest of the season. She wondered at that, though, then thought of all the calls from the broodmare owners. Probably he realized he'd lose most of the season moving the horse from one stud farm to another, and so had decided to leave Battle Cry here. That meant more breeding time available. And more stud fees.

"It figures," she said, refusing to admit she'd do the same if she were he.

Still, that was to her advantage. To house that fantastic horse in her stallion barn, even for half a season, would be a joy unduplicated. All she had to do was keep her response to James under control.

Anne groaned again.

The telephone rang, and she glared at it, knowing it had to be yet another owner looking to place his mare with Battle Cry. She schooled herself to patience and picked up the receiver.

"Hello?"

"What's all this Maida tells me about James and you and a horse?"

That her grandmother's voice was demanding wasn't surprising, Anne thought. That it had taken Lettice this long to find out about Battle Cry was. She grinned, thinking the state-of-the-art gossip line Lettice usually had had been a little slow on this one. Her grandmother must be fuming.

"James is boarding a horse with me," she said. "I told you before it was no big deal."

"In a pig's eye."

"Don't start, Grandmother," Anne warned. "I'm in no mood for a fight."

"You've said nothing about this . . . War Yell horse."

"Battle Cry."

"Whatever. You've said nothing about it, Anne. Now, why is that if it's no big deal?"

She clenched her teeth in an effort to hold her patience. Lettice was sniffing around like Tibbs on a rabbit hunt, and she was not about to be the rabbit. She had to convince Lettice there was nothing between her and James. "It wasn't my place to share this, Grandmother, it was James's. He owns the horse, not me. My business depends on *my* discretion. I hope you can understand that."

The dead silence on the other end of the line made Anne wonder if she'd gone too far. She loved her grandmother, but this truly wasn't Lettice's business. She was sorry if her grandmother didn't like it.

"I see. I see very well. . . ."

The speculative tone in her grandmother's voice was hardly the explosion of anger she'd been expecting. A shiver of apprehension ran down her spine.

"I find it very interesting that you preferred not to tell me about this."

"Grandmother, it's just a business arrangement," Anne said, as the prickles grew.

"Of course, child, of course. Maida just surprised me by having the news first. You know how I hate that. But that isn't why I called."

"It isn't?" Anne asked blankly.

"No, it isn't. I've arranged to have some work done on the house. It's absolutely necessary, and it must begin immediately. Unfortunately, I cannot stay here for the duration. The only suitable hotel used to be the Warwick, but now that's of-

fices. I certainly can't intrude on Ellen and Joe.
They're just married. I love my friends but I prefer
to live with family. Since you're the only family
close to the city, I've decided to stay with you. I'm
sure you'll agree that's the only solution."

Darkness closed in on Anne. The thought of
Lettice here was not to be thought. She took a
deep breath, trying desperately to come up with a
valid protest. "But, Grandmother—"

"Surely I'm welcome in my own granddaughter's house."

"Of course—"

"Fine, then that's settled. I'll make the final
arrangements and move my things over. It will be
for only six weeks."

"Six weeks!"

"Quite short for all the work being done here.
Thank you so much, my dear, for putting me up.
I feel so much better knowing I'll be with you. Oh!
And when I get there, you can tell me all about
this . . . business arrangement with James."

The line disconnected before Anne could say
anything more. She took the now-dead receiver
away from her ear and stared at it, deciding
Godzilla would be a more welcome guest. She knew
she'd been outmaneuvered. Lettice could outma-
neuver the slickest con man. She had a feeling
that even if she'd managed to get out a firm no, it
would have been completely ignored.

"Great," she muttered. "Just what I need."

She pulled herself upright. She could handle
having her grandmother here for a time. She had
to. Anyway, it wouldn't be too bad. Lettice's charity work was literally a full-time job. And she herself put in ten- to twelve-hour days at least, running

her farm. They'd probably pass each other only going to and from their bedrooms. She hoped.

Anne turned her mind to a bigger problem. James. She knew she must work with him. She would just have to remember his mercenary attitude toward Battle Cry. She had no doubt he'd help the situation by talking about his newfound equine profits every chance he got. From now on she would just keep the conversation away from breeding practices. A little horse sense about horse sex, she decided, and she'd be fine.

With a little luck.

Four

"He's here! He's here!"

Anne grinned in amusement as her son sped out of the house, Tibbs on his heels. One had to be listening very closely to hear the faint sound of a heavy-duty motor in the distance. Philip, excited from the moment he'd been told Battle Cry was retiring here, had been listening very closely.

She followed him more sedately, but that didn't stop her heart from pounding. As she stood on the portico, she told herself it was much too early for Battle Cry's transport van to have arrived. She didn't expect it until after noontime. But she stared up the long drive with growing anticipation.

First a car came into view. She recognized it instantly as James's Jaguar. Through the tinted windshield she could distinguish a silver-haired woman who looked like Lettice in the passenger seat. Following the car was a medium-size van with the legend ESCORT. QUALITY FURNITURE MOVERS on its side.

"It better not be," Anne muttered. Her grandmother had mentioned she planned to bring a few things when she came to stay. This was definitely *not* a few things!

The car pulled up in front of the house. James emerged and waved at her, before going around to the passenger side. Anne smiled back, hoping to show only politeness, not the burst of electricity frizzing along her nerve endings. He looked sensational in his pleated jeans and leather flight jacket, and her lungs seemed to lose all air as she stared at him. Her own worn jeans, old blue sweater, and sheepskin coat seemed dowdy rather than sensible now.

Fortunately, a more angry sizzle replaced the sensual one, as, sure enough, he helped Lettice out of the car. Lettice, nearly eighty now, had voluntarily retired herself from the roadways several years before. She had left Anne with the impression that she would hire a car when she was ready to come for her stay. She hadn't been expected today, let alone with James.

Wonderful, Anne thought. Now she had a Triple Crown winner and a grandmother to settle in at the same time. Not exactly her idea of a fun day.

"It's only Grandmother Lettice," Philip said with disappointment, then called out, "I thought you were Battle Cry, Grandmother Lettice!"

"You better not ever think I'm a horse, young man. I'll write you out of my will." She grinned at her great-grandson. "Now, come give me a kiss. I have a lot of things planned for us while I'm here."

Giggling, Philip ran down the steps and into her arms. Tibbs followed. The dog sat at Lettice's feet and whined like an unhappy puppy, until she deigned to scratch his ears.

"This is Mr. Tough Guy?" James asked as he joined Anne on the portico, jerking a thumb at the dog.

Fiery sensations flooded Anne's body at his closeness. She forced herself to ignore them, and scowled at the van instead. "Tibbs adores her. I have no idea why."

"I take it from Philip's remark that Battle Cry hasn't arrived yet?" James asked, the hope of a contradiction clear in his tone.

"Not yet," Anne said, grinning. "Why do I think that old saying about if wishes were horses is apt right now?"

He laughed. "Very apt, Annie. If it were true, there'd be a thousand Battle Crys on your doorstep."

She grimaced at the name Annie, but let it go. "If there were, then we wouldn't be this excited about one."

He chuckled, and Anne realized that their sharing a joke was as insidious to her control as him touching her. More. She could always excuse a physical response as just that. Nature's attraction circuits did not discriminate at times. But she couldn't dismiss emotional intimacy so easily. His generosity with her mare and his clear plan to keep the horse here through the breeding season confused her. He wasn't behaving quite like the James she thought she knew. She felt as if an invisible barrier were slowly and steadily crumbling inside her, and she had no idea how to shore it up again. The thought was disturbing.

She looked around for a distraction, and immediately found a second complication in her life to focus on. She had allowed her grandmother the time to greet Philip and Tibbs before confronting her over the van. It was more than enough time now. Excusing herself, Anne strode down the steps to Lettice.

"Grandmother, this is more than your necessities," she said when she reached her.

"I would prefer a kiss of hello for a greeting," Lettice said, all too clearly ready for a fight.

"Of course." Anne kissed her on the cheek, then laid down the law. "The men will unload only your clothes, your toiletries, your jewelry, and three things you absolutely *cannot* live without. The rest goes back to your place."

"Now, just one minute," Lettice began.

Anne cut her off. "I will be checking before the van leaves, and if you try to sneak in anything other than what I have just listed, it will be put back on the van. If you defy me and have everything moved in, I will have my people move everything back out, and they will be instructed to dump it on your front lawn. You are my guest, and as such I will treat you with gracious hospitality. I only ask the same of you, Madame."

Lettice stared regally at her. Nobody moved, nobody breathed in the stunned silence. All of them waited for the mega-ton explosion that was sure to come.

"Six things," Lettice finally said.

"Four," Anne countered.

"Five."

Anne smiled. "Four, and that's it. It was a nice try, Grandmother. Now cut your losses."

Lettice harrumphed, then turned to the moving men. "You heard my granddaughter, gentlemen."

"I warned you that you wouldn't get away with it," James said to Lettice as the men opened the back of the van.

"Don't be an 'I told you so,' James," she snapped

before going around to the back of the van to pick her four things.

Anne sighed with relief.

"Wow!" Philip exclaimed. "Nobody tells Grandmother Lettice what to do, Mom."

James grinned at her. "Nice shootin', Anne. You got her right in her good manners."

She grinned back. "I do feel like I just lived through the O.K. Corral."

Her gaze had been focused on his eyes. Now it began to wander, and she found it fixing on his mouth. She wondered what it would be like to feel his lips on hers again. Would they take her to a glorious paradise? Or would they fill her with a scorching heat? It had been so long since that one kiss between them. Part of her was terrified that she was even wondering, and part of her wanted to know the answers. . . .

"Boy, when's that horse getting here?" Philip asked, drawing his mother's attention. He stared up the drive.

"Yeah," James added. "When's that horse getting here?"

Relieved to be distracted from her traitorous body's response, Anne smothered a chuckle at the two of them. But her brain echoed the same thought. Now that she had settled with her grandmother, when the *hell* was that horse getting here?

Lettice regally marched up the steps, the moving men following her, loaded down with suitcases. "I know the way, Anne," she said, and swept into the house.

Anne grinned and glanced at James. Abruptly she realized they couldn't just stand there, staring at each other, while they waited for Battle

Cry. Her heart couldn't take it, for one thing. But the alternative of inviting James inside for coffee seemed too cozy. Not exactly the signal she wanted to send. Unfortunately, she had no choice without being rude.

Screwing up her courage, she asked, "Would you like coffee while we wait?"

His smile almost melted her. "I'd love it."

They went inside. She was all too aware of James walking directly behind her, his steps matching hers. It reminded her of a big cat stalking its prey . . . patient, watchful . . . all that power under control . . . waiting for the right moment to reach out and take . . .

The kitchen, with its everyday utensils, brought a needed dose of common sense to her unruly imagination. James might be an attractive man, but he was just a man. Getting involved with him would be a mistake. She'd already made one, and she wasn't about to make another.

She poured them both coffee and settled across the kitchen table from him. He said nothing, but simply gazed at her, his eyes pinning her. Her face heated, and she couldn't quite catch her breath. His gaze lowered to her breasts. Her nipples tightened.

Move, she told herself. Say something. But her body was melting under his hot, sensual gaze, and she wanted nothing more than for him to reach out and touch her, kiss her. . . .

Philip skipped into the kitchen, chattering away. "Grandmother Lettice says she'll take me to the art museum and to see the dinosaurs. . . ."

Anne flopped back in her chair, released from the sensual purgatory James had created within her with just one look. One look! She was in deep trouble.

"Get Lettice to take you through the armory room at the museum," James said, sounding completely uneffected. "They have weapons over two thousand years old."

"Really excellent!" Philip exclaimed.

As the two of them discussed war gear through the ages, a vague uneasiness settled over Anne. James seemed to enjoy talking to Philip. She would have thought he wouldn't be bothered with a child. But far from condescending, he was genuinely interested in Philip's opinions. And Philip was clinging to every word. Enjoying children was a side of James she hadn't expected. The image she'd had of him slipped further off its pedestal, leaving her even more confused.

They no sooner finished their coffee when a second van was heard roaring along the drive. Philip spoke for the adults when he shouted, "Finally!"

They all hurried back outside. The drivers had been sent a map with instructions on where to unload the horse. Clearly, a mixup had occurred, and to Anne's horror she watched the van take the right turn off the circular drive toward the mares' stables, not left toward the stallion barn.

"Stop!" she screamed, waving and running toward the van. "Not that way!"

"Not that way!" Philip shouted, his tone echoing his mother's panic.

The driver waved back, and she realized he'd taken both her and her son's motions for a welcoming. The windows of the cab were rolled up and the man couldn't hear her. The van continued on around the drive. Anne ran after them, her son running with her. Most of the mares were in heat, and there'd be hell to pay when the stallion got within scent of them.

"Why are we running?" James asked, jogging up alongside her.

"That's the mares' stables," Philip said, panting. "The horses'll all go crazy if they're put together. We gotta stop them before they get too close. Otherwise, Battle Cry'll go nuts."

Anne was grateful her son had answered. She didn't want to waste the breath. All of them ran faster.

They were too late. They arrived at the first courtyard of the mares' stables to hear clattering hooves and something heavy banging against the inside walls of the horse van. This was topped by loud whinnying and human curses, also from inside the van. From the stables came dozens of answering whinnies and more banging, while the mares in the paddocks outside were running restlessly, their foals at their sides. Her people were scurrying around, trying to calm the animals, but nature was having its own fireworks show. Nothing but distance would stop it.

"Dammit! Move that van!" Anne shouted as the driver and an assistant simultaneously opened the cab doors. "Follow the drive all the way around. Now, move it!"

"But . . . but . . ."

"You heard the lady," James roared. "Move that van!"

The men slammed the doors shut in hasty compliance. From the back of the van she heard "About bloody damn time!"

With a screech of tires, the van zoomed off

around the rest of the drive. Her face heated from the run and from embarrassment, Anne was relieved to see it go . . . and resentful that it had taken James to get the driver to pay attention. After all, she was the owner of the farm, not he. She had always hated not being taken seriously—she had even quit racing when she discovered the other jockeys "eased up" on her because she was a woman. She could never be sure she had truly won a race, or if the men hadn't ridden all-out against her. And yet she was in a male-dominated business. Sometimes she just had to grit her teeth and accept help from "the great big man." Still, the whole incident was humiliating. James was probably thinking she was a nincompoop. She wished she could start the day over and make a much better impression with him.

Otis, her head groom for the mares, strode over to her. "Who was the idiot who did that?" he demanded.

The idiot wasn't important. The mares were. Concerned, Anne asked, "What about the mares, Otis? Do you think this upset them too much?"

"Probably not as much as it upset the stallion. The mares should be okay. They're calming down now." They could hear the panicked whinnying and restlessness abating. Otis chuckled. "Poor Battle Cry. He probably thought it was a deliberate torture to smell all the ladies and be trapped inside that little bitty box."

Anne couldn't help grinning at his description. Otis was small and dark and had a knack for knowing when the mares would be most receptive to a stallion. She was lucky to have him, and she knew it.

Philip tugged at her sleeve. "Mom? Can we go see Battle Cry now?"

"Yeah," James said, grinning excitedly. "Can we?"

Anne smiled at him. She couldn't have stopped the smile if she tried. And she didn't want to try.

"Go, go, Anne," Otis said, shooing her with one hand. "Your mares will be fine. Go see to their new husband."

With a last wave they were again on the run.

James glanced at the woman next to him with a mixture of admiration, tenderness . . . and lust. Annie Kitteridge was something, he thought. She'd gone toe to toe with her grandmother, and that had taken quite a bit of courage. Truthfully, he wouldn't want to face down Lettice. Then Anne had been ready to take the van driver apart for his mistake, and in the next breath was genuinely concerned for the well-being of her mares. Now she was ready to handle the arrival of a prized and very touchy stallion.

He noted her face was flushed, her jaw set with determination, yet that look only made her seem young and vulnerable, just as he remembered her from that summer long ago. His heart twisted. She moved with a grace a dancer would envy, and her light scent, like clover on a dewy morning, spun enticingly through his senses. She challenged a man to break through the steel and find the softly petaled rose underneath.

"All these horses," he said breathlessly as they jogged between the fenced pastures. "And we're running like Carl Lewis on the five hundred."

"I prefer Flo-Jo," Anne said. She laughed. "I'd say Battle Cry is pretty free of quirks, wouldn't you?"

"And loving the idea of retirement," he added, grinning at her.

She blushed and glanced at her son. James realized it might not have been a good remark to make in front of Philip, but the boy was already pulling ahead of them, his attention obviously on getting to the barn first. James liked the boy. Philip had the same look of determination as his mother, combined with a child's excitement. He knew exactly how the boy felt.

They arrived at the stallion barn just in time to see the back of the van opened and the ramp being laid out. Inside the dim interior a robe-covered horse was still prancing restlessly, but not frantic enough to burst its restraints.

"I heard," were the first words from Anne's head stallion groom, Curtis.

Anne nodded to the tall young man. James had missed Curtis on his first visit to the farm. As he was introduced, he decided the man was a little too tall and too young for his liking. Also, he gazed at Anne with a proprietary look that James didn't care for. Even knowing he had no claim on her, James was bothered by Curtis more than he cared to admit.

"When he calms enough to back him out of the van," Anne said briskly to Curtis, "put him into one of the paddocks. He can run the rest of his excitement off there."

"Right."

Curtis was a man of few words, James observed.

The first thing out of the transport van was not Battle Cry, but a small gray-haired man who immediately turned on the hapless driver and his assistant.

"You nearly sent my boy to the glue factory!" he shouted, not at all sounding like their coworker. "What the hell happened back there?"

The two men nearly fell all over themselves trying to explain about misreading the map. The gray-haired man glowered ominously, then snorted. "If there's any damage to my boy, I'll see everyone here sues your company for giving us two of the biggest dummies the good Lord created!"

"Excuse me," Anne said, frowning at him. "I'm Anne Kitteridge, the owner of Makefield Meadows."

He turned and appraised her, then smiled and shook her hand. "I've seen you race, miss. You were a fine rider in your day. And you're making quite a name for yourself with this farm."

"Thank you," Anne said, smiling at his compliment.

Before she could say more, he turned to James.

"And you must be Mr. Farraday." The man grinned, his anger gone like lightning. He grabbed James's hand and pumped it vigorously. For a small man his fingers were surprisingly strong. "I'm Oliver MacGinley—Mac to ya. I saw you when you came out to see Battle Cry several months ago, although you probably don't remember seeing me. Now you're the new owner of my boy. That's wonderful, wonderful, sir. I work for Riker Racing Stables, Battle Cry's trainer. I've had the pleasure of taking care of my boy since he left his mama. Oh!" He reached into his pocket and produced several papers. "Here's the paperwork."

"I'm very pleased to meet you," James said. He took the papers from Mac and shoved them into his pocket without a glance. He tried to remember the man from his trip last fall to Riker, but gave up. The place had been huge, after all. "Did he make the trip all right? We've been a little worried about that."

"Set your mind at ease, sir. He's a good traveler. Except when he's taken to the wrong kind of stables by a couple of . . . Never mind."

James chuckled. "Your hard work made him a winner."

Mac nodded. "That it did, if I may say so. Many long hours I put in schooling him—"

A stamping and a loud whinny interrupted Mac, who seemed to jump at a hidden command.

"That's my boy wanting out of his cage." The man scurried back up the van ramp, calling over his shoulder. "You'll be wanting to see him anyway. I'm forgetting my manners, sir and good lady. I won't be needin' no help," he added suddenly to Curtis, who moved toward the van. "My boy will come out like a lamb, you'll see."

The man definitely had charm, James thought as Mac disappeared into the van's interior. Especially with his manner of formal speech. Somewhere, too, was a hint of a long-ago brogue. He refused to admit, however, that Curtis's angry expression at being reprimanded had any influence on his opinion of Mac.

He glanced over at Anne to find her looking worried. He wished he could wipe away all of her concerns, whatever they were. His surge of protectiveness wasn't good, he knew. It meant there was more than chemistry at work. He'd have to be much more careful from now on.

The horse came out just then, with a last little prance of hooves. Mac unclipped the blue robe, whisking it off Battle Cry's broad back, then led the animal over to a paddock. He regally allowed Curtis to hold open the gate before he unclipped the rope lead and slapped Battle Cry into the pasture. With a snort of startlement, the horse leapt forward like a well-oiled machine coming to life. Curtis shut the gate, and all the humans walked over to the fence and leaned on it, watching in reverent silence.

Battle Cry was breathtaking. He was a true bay with a white blaze down his forehead. His ears flicked with intelligence, the eyes were almost fiery with an inner life force. The deep reddish-brown hide gleamed with vitality and covered a streamlined body of solid bone and muscle. He galloped around the enclosure with a grace that was pure pleasure to see.

"Wow," Philip said in awe, speaking for all the adults.

"He's beautiful," Anne said, her voice dreamy. She leaned her forearms along the top rail and rested her chin in her fist.

"I knew it would be like this," James murmured, watching her watch the horse. Nothing in the world would ever give him more pleasure than this moment. He had spent a whopping amount of money to get Battle Cry, and it didn't matter a damn. He felt honored just to be in the horse's presence. Furthering his line would bring a wild beauty into the world that no money could buy. Anne understood all of that, he knew. It was why he had been so desperate to share this with her. Louder, he said, "He looks happy in his new home."

"Hardly fretting, but no thanks to those nitwits," Mac muttered ominously, then added, "So you all like my boy."

Anne smiled at him. "You've kept him in good health, Mac."

To James's amusement, Curtis nodded grudgingly.

"It's my job, miss." Mac stared at the horse and sighed. "That was my job. Who will have his care now?"

"All of us share the duties," Curtis said.

The man straightened. "But he hates a lot of different people touching him! You'll upset him, make him unhappy—"

"His whole routine will be different now," Anne said, her voice soothing. "It will be very hard on him, I know, and he'll miss you. But we'll be extra good to him, Mac. We know how to help a horse adjust to a new environment. You come back in a few weeks and it'll be as if he's always been here."

James could hear the sympathy in her voice. He felt bad, too, for the man. That Battle Cry would adjust he was sure. It was Mac he wasn't sure of, and he felt responsible for causing this unhappiness.

"I don't doubt you'll take good care of him," Mac said, "and I mean no insult. But you don't know his quirks. Ya wouldn't have an opening for a groom, miss, would you? I'll just take care of my boy, I promise. I'll just see to his personal needs. Everything else up to your people, of course. I wouldn't interfere, miss, and you'll only have to pay me room and board."

Anne smiled gently. "I'm sorry. I have all the grooms I need right now."

"Mom!" Philip looked stricken at her words.

The life seemed to go out of the little man, although he straightened with dignity. "I . . . I was hoping. But I can't say I didn't expect ya to refuse. Oh, well. Riker's planning to retire me, too, when I get back. Not looking forward to it. Can't turn off the horses, can we?"

Overwhelming guilt assailed James at the man's words, and he couldn't stand it. It was clear the man was devoted to the horse, and he was being pulled apart by the thought of separation. In fact, his entire world was crumbling, and all because he, James, had bought a horse. It was through Mac's care that Battle Cry had arrived so safely, and he was grateful. More than grateful. What Anne must be thinking of him for creating this mess . . .

"I'll pay his salary and room and board, Anne," he volunteered. "You know that's no problem. Can he be my employee here to oversee my horse?"

Mac nearly jumped with joy, then looked at Anne hopefully. She glared at James, who knew she had a right to.

"James, I'm sympathetic to Mac," she said. "We're all horsepeople, and we know how he feels."

"He'll facilitate Battle Cry's adjustment," James said, his enthusiasm growing. "After all, he knows the horse better than anyone else." He turned to Curtis and the other grooms. "I know you men will take good care of my horse. Don't you think, though, that Mac could help with his transition here?"

The men stared at him. Curtis finally said, "It's up to Anne."

James turned back to her. "Can we try it? For two weeks?"

She said nothing, just looked at him.

James realized belatedly he was putting her in an awkward position. Still, he liked the idea of

Mac helping Battle Cry through the first few weeks at the farm, and if it worked out . . . well, maybe a permanent arrangement could be made. He would feel awful if he didn't help this old man who clearly loved the horse as if it were his own family. "I know I'm putting you on the spot, Anne, but if he keeps only to the grooming and feeding of Battle Cry, how about it? The least little complaint from you or your men, and I'll fire him. Agreed, Mac?"

"I'll be no trouble, sir. Honest, miss. Your men will know my boy's business best now. I'll do whatever they ask of me."

Anne stared at Mac, clearly assessing the man's character, trying to discern if it matched his words. She glanced at her men, all of them impassive. James waited impatiently.

"Two weeks," she finally said.

Mac cheered, tears actually starting in his eyes. He took her hand and shook it. "You won't be sorry, miss. None of you will. I promise."

James grinned when the little man turned to him. His hand was pumped until he was afraid it would be shaken off his arm.

"Thank you, sir. Bless you. I'll do a good job for you, you'll see."

When his hand was finally released, James turned to thank Anne for her generous decision. But she was already halfway down the drive toward the house. Her ramrod-straight back made it all too clear how she felt. Mac was too ecstatic to notice, and her employees were drifting back to their usual work. He admitted none of them looked too happy either. He sighed, knowing he had overstepped himself.

"I think Mom's mad," Philip said, looking up at

James. "But I'm kinda glad you talked her into it."

James smiled dryly. "So am I."

Leaving Mac content to look at his "boy," James walked with Philip back to the house. Lettice was waiting on the portico.

"My granddaughter just stomped into the house, cursing faster than a sailor," she said. "She was cursing you, James. What did you do to become persona non grata?"

He shrugged noncommittally. He wasn't about to tell Lettice what happened. Besides, it wasn't her business. But it looked as if he'd made more of a mistake with Anne than he'd first thought.

He'd made a biggie.

Five

"Really, Anne. He was right, so why don't you just admit it and speak to the man? Five days of avoiding him is quite enough punishment."

Anne took a deep breath to hold her patience and set her spoonful of cereal back into her bowl. She would *not* argue this point at breakfast.

"I haven't been avoiding him, Grandmother," she said in as reasonable a tone as she could muster. "Anyway, I agreed with James when I said Mac could stay, so I don't see the point of this conversation."

"Well, I do," Lettice replied bluntly. "You won't speak to James."

"Keep this up, and I won't speak to you," Anne said, picking up her spoon again. She stared at Lettice as she ate her cereal.

Lettice stared back.

"Grandmother Lettice, can we go to the zoo this Saturday?" Philip asked into the silence.

Lettice grimaced at being the first to break the

eye-to-eye showdown. "Yes, Philip. If you like, I can get us in early to see the baby rhino—"

Anne took the opportunity to escape. She was out the door to begin her morning rounds of the stables before Lettice had finished answering Philip. Her son's timing was perfect.

"What a way to start a day," she murmured, sighing. She wished she had never told Lettice what had happened. While her grandmother sided with her, she also seemed to want all the "bygones be bygones" to come from her granddaughter. Bygones when she was furious with him? In a pig's eye! Anne had no desire to speak to the man except for business purposes, and she'd be damned before she did.

Still, she never would have expected him to hire Mac like that. Sympathetic maybe, but not so . . . nice. She walked faster, her steps angry. He had done something kind, proving yet again that he was Mr. Perfect, and had usurped her authority at the same time.

The day, unfortunately, went from bad to worse.

"Anne, I want to talk to you."

She took a deep breath as James blocked her path to the foaling stable. For five days he had made the same demand—when he could find her. This time, though, she was ready for him. This would be a business conversation whether he liked it or not. What else did he want from her anyway?

"I have something for you." She slipped some papers from her clipboard and held them out to him. The afternoon sun was in her eyes, but she refused to shade them to see him more clearly. Still, her brain registered that he looked as sexy as ever, and she was disgusted with herself for even being interested. She remembered figuring he'd show up at the farm only every couple of months or so to see his horse. So far he'd been there every day.

"This is Battle Cry's breeding schedule," she said, and instantly realized her mistake. Breeding was the last thing she wanted to discuss with him.

He took the papers from her, their fingers somehow not touching in the process. Anne ignored the disappointment of her body. James stuffed the schedule in the inside pocket of his corduroy jacket.

"Aren't you going to look it over?" she asked, shock momentarily overriding her reaction to him.

"I trust you to know your business." His gaze hardened. "Besides, I know this is an attempt to change the subject."

Anne glowered back at him. Her fury was refueled at his not looking over the schedule. "If the subject is Mac, I told you before there's nothing to talk about. You own Battle Cry. You want Mac to take care of him. I agreed."

"We haven't talked at all," he began. "You haven't allowed me a word—"

"You had plenty to say when your horse arrived. Do you want to take any of it back?"

His face darkened. "No."

She smiled sweetly. "Fine. Now, if you'll excuse me—"

"No." He practically straddled the walking path. "I know I put you in a very awkward position—"

"Yes, you did," she interrupted. "But that didn't stop you, did it? *Nobody* felt worse than I did when I had to say no. But I have other employees whose jobs were usurped by your demand that I employ Mac as Battle Cry's personal groom—"

"Dammit, I didn't demand."

"You left me no choice, James," she said, her anger boiling over. "You even insured I looked like an ogre to my own son. Next time if you don't like one of my decisions, please discuss it with me *in private.* I do try to accommodate the horses' owners as best I can. I have bowed to your wishes, James. We have nothing further to say, and I will not discuss this again with you. Now, I have three mares in labor to see to, and no, you cannot come along. Strangers can upset them and endanger their foals."

She walked around him and on up the path. When she didn't hear his footsteps behind her, she allowed herself to relax. Clearly, he believed her about the mares.

Good, she thought murderously. Her temper frayed at each meeting with him since this business with Mac. It still rankled her that James had embarrassed her in front of her employees and her son by putting her in an untenable position. She was grateful her people had realized that, although she was receiving the cool shoulder from a few for her allowing Mac to stay. Philip had forgotten the incident already, as children did.

At least Mac was sticking faithfully to their agreement and caring only for the horse's personal needs. Curtis said he was friendly and helpful, fitting himself into the routine of the stallions. That news relieved her anxieties. It irritated her too. She would have felt a certain pleasure in telling James *his* employee was not working out.

But Mr. Perfect had done the perfect thing again. If only he hadn't made her into the Witch of Makefield Meadows in the process. It hurt more than she cared to admit. More, perhaps, than it should.

Probably she was holding on to her anger because he was around the farm so damn much these days. She couldn't turn around without seeing him, and had taken to avoiding the stallion barn.

As she entered the foaling stable, she wondered if she had somehow been getting her hopes up about James. Impossible, she decided. She had learned her lesson years before. All she needed to learn now was how to stay on a professional footing with him. Completely professional. No more wanting to be pulled into his arms, no more urges to be kissed breathless as she had when she'd been seventeen. Certainly no more desire . . .

"You look about ready to foal yourself, Anne," Jonas said.

She mentally shook away her disturbing thoughts and smiled at the man in charge of bringing new life into the world. "It's been a long day. How are my mares?"

"All progressing nicely. No complications so far. Come along and see them."

She followed Jonas past several unoccupied stalls to the far end of the stables.

"I'm keeping them down this end," he said. "I have a feeling they're going to deliver assembly-line style."

Anne leaned on a stall's half door. The dark mare inside was lying down, a sure sign of advanced labor. The animal looked placid, though, as if a momentous occurrence was the last thing about to happen. Anne smiled in pleasure, her heart filling at the prospect of another spindly-legged baby romping in her pastures.

Then she remembered the man outside the building. She wouldn't be surprised if James were waiting for her to come out to resume the "discussion."

"Mind if I hang around for a while?" she asked Jonas.

He chuckled. "You're the boss."

"I like to think so," she muttered, and turned back to the mare.

James strode toward the house and his car, his teeth clenched with frustration.

He visited Battle Cry every day, and he had tried to apologize every time he saw Anne. And every damn time she managed to prevent him from doing so. She must have taken lessons from her grandmother, he decided. Or else it was in the genes. Whatever, Anne had that regal eye and imperious tone of Lettice's. Combined with her refusal to back down, she had been a stone wall that he hadn't been able to chip. It was as if she didn't want to hear an apology from him. He couldn't understand her.

One thing he understood, however, was his re-action to her. His own anger had combined with a more primitive urge, and every time he saw her he wanted to grab her and kiss her senseless. He couldn't keep his mind on anything else lately. A part of him had been empty for so long. He hadn't realized until he'd seen her at the polo match how he had walled his emotions over.

Anne Kitteridge was driving him insane.

He was passing a group of bushes near the mares' stables when he saw Philip standing on the bottom rail of a fence, feeding carrots to sev-eral mares in the pasture. James thought to pass him with just a wave, then he heard an unhappy sniffling sound. Philip was crying. He hesitated for a moment, then walked over to the boy.

"Hi," he said, leaning against the fence.

"Hi."

Philip ducked his head and surreptitiously swiped at his face. James hid a smile. The mares had moved away for an instant at the sight and smell of a stranger, but the lure of a treat brought them back. Their foals, more cautious with new-born instinct, hovered behind the mothers.

"Can I have a carrot?" James asked.

Philip passed one over, and he broke it into chunks and fed it to two of the mares.

"I hope I'm not disturbing you," he said. "It's nice to just watch the late afternoon sun turn red with someone, although sometimes, too, a person likes to be alone and think. You look like you have things to think about."

"I . . . it's okay," Philip said. "You can stay."

The boy shared the rest of the carrots with him, and the two of them fed the horses and watched the sun set. James didn't ask any questions, sensing Philip wanted to say something, but wouldn't if probed. He realized it must be hard for the boy, with his father on the other side of the country.

Finally Philip said, "I hate bullies."

James considered the comment, then said, "So do I. I used to get picked on a lot when I was a kid." He grinned. "Now I'm bigger and richer than they are."

"I didn't hear the teacher today," Philip said, unmollified. "Just 'cause I—"

The boy stopped, and James knew instantly what was wrong. Suddenly he was whisked back to his own childhood.

"Because you wear a hearing aid, the kids tease you sometimes," he said gravely.

"Just one kid," Philip said, then added the devastating blow. "But even my friends laughed."

"I see." James was silent for a moment. "Sometimes people laugh without realizing a person's feelings are being hurt, or they laugh because everyone else is and they're embarrassed to be different."

"Yeah, maybe I should hurt their feelings or make people laugh at them."

"You might be hurting yourself in the end," James warned. "It's not fair, I know. Sometimes things just aren't fair."

"That's really stupid," Philip said, his voice filled with resentment. "You wouldn't say that if people laughed and called you dummy because you wore a hearing aid."

"Yes, I would." James took a deep breath, amazed that he was about to tell this boy the secret he had kept from so many others for so many years. The secret he had kept from Anne, out of fear. "When I was your age people called me dummy because I couldn't read. My friends laughed. I was so angry that I hurt them back, and wound up getting more hurt in the end."

"You . . ." Philip stared at him. "You couldn't read?"

"I have a learning disability called dyslexia, Philip." He patted his pockets for something to prove his point, but the only thing readable was the schedule Anne had given him. He removed it from his pocket and looked it over carefully, just to make sure the schedule was nothing but names and dates. He held it out. "I don't see letters and numbers the way most people do. Here, read the first line or so of this for me."

Philip quickly read the first few lines out loud, only stumbling over one of the horses' names. Constitution's Preamble would be a tongue twister for most nine-year-olds.

"When I was your age," James said, retrieving the schedule, "I couldn't have even read that. The letters would look all mixed up. I've learned how to overcome it pretty well. But even now, when I'm tired or angry or distracted, I'll make mistakes."

"Would you like me to read the rest for you, Mr. Farraday?" Philip offered.

He smiled and tucked the papers back into his pocket. "Thanks, but I'm okay now. One of the things that helped me with bullies was to laugh at their jokes, too, along with everyone else. It hurt at first, but they didn't like it that their victim was laughing and joking around with them. After a while they stopped teasing me."

"I'll remember that." The boy looked away. "Don't tell my mom I was . . . they were teasing me. It really upsets her, and she gets mad at my friends and the school."

"I respect your privacy, Philip, so I won't discuss this conversation with anyone." James could imagine how Anne would react with a mother's protectiveness, which was the kiss of death to a nine-year-old boy.

Philip straightened. "I won't discuss it, Mr. Farraday."

"James."

Philip smiled. "James."

James realized that Philip's impairment had an advantage over his own. The hearing aid made it visible early on to people. His dyslexia was easy to hide. People wouldn't know until he chose to tell them, and it had become a lifetime habit to choose not to.

He had been one of the unlucky ones, and hadn't been diagnosed early. Instead, he'd been labeled disruptive and lazy, and had been sent away to military school to "shape up." Finally one of his teachers had realized he needed help, and eventually he'd overcome the dyslexia.

Still, the emotional scars had remained until college. It had been a small college, but just getting in had done much for his low self-esteem. His socially conscious parents, unsupportive as ever, hadn't wanted him to sully the family name by failing. He'd gone anyway. He'd even gotten engaged in his senior year to a "deb." And he'd confessed, with a laugh, his dyslexia. Unfortunately, she hadn't laughed. Instead, she'd broken off the engagement because she didn't want to have "problem" children.

He had come home that summer so embittered. He'd known he could never open himself again to a woman. And then on impulse he had kissed seventeen-year-old Annie Kitteridge at a dance . . . and had realized that whatever he'd felt for the deb had been nothing compared to what he'd felt in that instant with Anne. Life, with its wry sense of timing, had really shown him what he could never have. Anne had left shortly afterward for the racing world she loved, and he was never sure if he should have been grateful or angry with her for doing so.

"It's almost dinnertime," Philip said. "Would you like to stay for dinner if it's okay with Grandmother Lettice? She's cooking tonight. Sometimes the owners stay."

He thought of his earlier reaction to Anne, of her coolness to him. What was the sense of staying when nothing could be changed? Truthfully, she was treating him like a business associate, and he ought to accept it. That was all he'd wanted when he'd offered her Battle Cry.

"Sure," he said with a grin. "I'll stay."

By the time Anne left the stable after ten o'clock, three new foals had come into the world. Jonas had been right on target, she thought, stretching her arms over her head. All three mares had delivered in classic assembly-line procedure—with no complications. Smiling, she admitted she liked that best of all.

Although she'd missed dinner and was feeling tired, she decided to take the long route to the house by way of the stallion barn and breeding shed. A few steps farther to enjoy a brilliant spring night sky wouldn't hurt.

She wondered if James would be there tomorrow, and immediately stopped herself. She refused to think about him again. He was the owner of one of her horses, that was all. She'd been living on one lousy kiss too long.

She tried to keep her mind on the business of tomorrow—Battle Cry's first mating. They'd allowed him these past days to adjust to his new surroundings, and he certainly seemed content. He was eating well, running the pastures, and accepting treats from the various people who would be involved in his new "profession." Otis felt Lollipop was ready, and Curtis had told her Battle Cry was itching to go. Tomorrow was the big test.

As she passed the darkened stallion barn, Anne grinned. She hoped Battle Cry would prove to be a "happy camper" in his retirement and accept all the mares sent to him.

The breeding shed loomed on her left, and she remembered being in there with James. It had taken every ounce of her willpower to resist the urges that had run through her that morning. Lord, how she had wanted him. But, she told herself, she didn't want him now.

Hoping to head off her dangerous thoughts yet again, she decided to check the lock on the breeding shed. An employee was assigned to stay in the animals' buildings each night, but head grooms were responsible for locking up the various sheds. She trusted them, but whenever she was on the grounds late she liked to double-check for her own peace of mind. To her satisfaction, the lock was secure when she tugged on it.

"Anne."

Shrieking, she leapt around at the sound of her name. The broad silhouette towering over her turned out to be James.

"What the hell are you trying to do, sneaking up on me like that?" she demanded, her heart racing with residual fear.

"I was looking for you," he said. "You didn't come in for dinner."

"I didn't . . ." She forced back a wave of shock. "You stayed for dinner?"

"Philip asked me. With Lettice's permission. They didn't seem worried that you were late. But I thought I would check."

"They know to start without me," she said. "This isn't a nine-to-five job."

"I thought I would just check."

"I . . . thank you." She didn't know what else to say without sounding like the Witch of Makefield Meadows again. And his concern was surprising . . . and touching.

Anne swallowed. She didn't need touching.

"Can we talk, Annie?" he asked, coming impossibly closer with just one step.

She tried to breathe normally, but her lungs weren't receiving nearly enough air.

"We talked already," she replied, her voice sounding faint.

"I'm sorry for what I did," he whispered. "Why can't you accept my apology?"

She backed up until the wall of the shed was solid against her shoulder blades. It put only three steps between them. Three were better than nothing on a starlit spring night, she rationalized.

"I accepted it, James. That's why there's nothing more to say about Mac."

"You were . . . friendlier before I asked you to take him on."

"I said I accepted. I didn't say I had to like it."

The words hung in the air between them, a challenge to their mutual control. Anne was all too aware of his hard body. The mingled scents of subtle cologne and horses teased her senses. She could hear his breath coming heavily, as if he, too, couldn't get enough air into his lungs.

"You make me crazy, Anne."

"I don't want to."

His hand reached out, his fingers lightly tracing her cheek. She felt as if she were being burned, yet she couldn't pull away.

"You make me more than crazy," he whispered, taking those last steps. Darkness seemed to envelop them in a black cocoon.

"Don't," she said when his chest just touched her breasts. Her nipples tightened into aching points at the contact.

"Don't what?" he asked, his hand curving around her throat in a gentle caress. Her skin felt like silk under his fingers.

"Don't do this. Don't kiss me like you did before."

"I'll kiss you better," he promised.

His mouth covered hers. She knew she should pull away, walk away, run away. But her own reason was gone at the feel of his lips on hers again. She was already being dragged over that remembered cliff and into a sensual fire unlike any she had experienced before . . . or since. How could he do it again? And why, she wondered dimly, why was James Farraday the only one who could do this to her?

But instinct took over, and she was lost to the kiss. She wound her arms around his shoulders, feeling the strength in them. Their mouths melded together eagerly, her body tight against his. She wasn't sure whether it was his hands on her back that urged her closer, or her own want riding her.

Hands pushed clothing away to find the warm flesh of man and woman. He cupped her breasts, his fingers exploring every inch of the soft skin. She moaned into his mouth when he brought her nipples to exquisite aching points.

The feel of his hard muscles flexing under her hands sent her mind and body spinning with desire. She raked her nails lightly across his back and felt the shiver run deep through him. Some hidden knowledge told her how to move and touch to bring him the most pleasure. It was as if she had touched him since the dawn of time. The rightness of being with him like this was undeniable.

She gasped for air when his mouth left hers to trail hot kisses over her cheeks, her jaw, her throat.

"Lord help me, but I want you, Annie Kitteridge," he murmured against her shoulder. He lifted his head and stepped away. "But I won't have you."

"What?" She sagged against the shed wall, her

arms empty. Her ears rang with his unbelievable words.

"It's the wrong time and the wrong place," he said, turning away. "I wasn't fair. I'm sorry, Anne."

"Do you always have to do the perfect thing?" she asked, pain lancing through her at his rejection. And why did she always have to be on the receiving end when he did? The humiliation was unbearable.

"What are you talking about?" he asked, his bewilderment clear.

"Nothing," she muttered, straightening. She pushed her clothes back into place. "Nothing. Thank you, James, for coming to *our* senses. I promise you this will not happen again."

Before he could say another word, she walked away from him.

James watched her go. He let her go. It would always be the wrong time and the wrong place.

Six

"... if the projected figures are right, we stand to make our original investment back three hundred percent ..."

The voice droned on and on, the speaker's tone dull and muted in the small wood-paneled conference room. James stared at the papers before him. They could have been written in Greek for all he was interested in them. And he ought to be. He was asking these people to make a sizable investment. Instead, he found himself thinking of Anne.

It was all too easy to invoke memories of last night's kiss. He hadn't meant to kiss her. But her closeness, her lithe body, and the elusive scent of her that he'd remembered all too well over the years had combined into an irresistible aphrodisiac. He could still feel her mouth sweet and intoxicating against his. Her flesh had been like expensive satin under his hands. Her body had been a perfect fit to his. He had forgotten all the reasons that anything between them was impossible. Even now, those reasons seemed to fade. . . .

"What do you think, James?"

He sat up in the leather wing chair and tried to look as if he knew what he was supposed to be thinking. He cleared his throat. "I think everything ought to be considered."

The three men and two women stared at him in bewilderment. Obviously, he wasn't to consider anything. He grinned ruefully.

"Good thing I wasn't driving, folks. Now, what was the full question?"

His prospective investors chuckled, and the question was restated. As James gave his opinion on a payment schedule, he decided it would be wisest to stay away from the farm today.

Four hours later, James turned his Jaguar into Anne's long drive. Despite his earlier thoughts, he told himself he did have a right to see his horse. After all, Battle Cry was being bred today—for the first time ever. A horse ought to have a little support from his owner on such a special occasion.

He parked his car in front of the house. Nobody was about, not even the dog. He frowned and loosened his tie. A three-piece suit wasn't the most sensible clothing for a horse farm. Deciding to leave his jacket on against the cool day, he got out of the car . . . and immediately faced Anne as she opened the front door.

He tensed. At that moment he realized that despite the feelings the kiss had provoked, nothing had changed for him. He could never tell her; he could never accept a rejection from her. From another woman maybe, but not from Anne. His instincts had been right all those years earlier, and they were telling him the same thing again.

Her expression went from smiling to closed the moment she spotted him. It hurt to know she responded to him with her body, yet not with her mind. It hurt even more to know he was responding to her the way he always did—with instant want. Within him there was a place that only she was capable of touching.

"Hello," she said, closing the front door behind her. She stood in front of it, unmoving.

"Hi." He couldn't find anything else to say. Finally he remembered his reason for coming. He removed his sunglasses and tucked them into his jacket pocket. "How did it go with Battle Cry and Lollipop's Rainbow?"

"Ah . . . fine. Fine." Her gaze shifted away from him.

"I just thought I'd come by and check—" He stopped. He'd been "checking" last night when he'd come upon her by the breeding shed. Maybe the location had effected his libido. Then again, maybe not, he decided as he stared into her wide blue-green eyes. "No problems?"

"No, everything was . . . it was . . ." She shrugged and glanced away, clearly uncomfortable in his presence. "Why don't you go up and see him?"

"Sure." He looked down in an effort to break the strange tension between them. He hadn't felt this awkward since his first lesson at dancing school. "I . . . How's Mac working out?"

As soon as the question left his lips, he knew it was a mistake. Mac was a sore topic between them. But to his surprise, she said only, "Fine." The lack of anger in her tone signaled that fight was ended. Or at least in the background.

But it was disheartening to realize they were like strangers forced into each other's company.

Previously, a spark of . . . something had existed between them. Now even that seemed to be gone.

"I'm glad everything went well with the horses," he said.

She nodded.

He stared at her a moment longer, memorizing her face, then turned and walked away.

She couldn't stand it any longer.

Anne stalked toward the stallion barn. James had kissed her three days ago, and she hated herself for still thinking of it. Every meeting with him was more and more awkward. If she'd been avoiding him before, she was trying to disappear now. It seemed like days since she'd looked at her stallions, but this was the first opportunity she'd had. James had almost been living there. Earlier, though, she had seen him heading for the house and his car, so she'd come over when she was finished in the foaling stable.

She was truly grateful to him for stopping the kiss before it got further out of hand. Or before being further in hand, she thought, remembering the way he had touched her. Yes, she *was* grateful. She could never be the kind of woman she was certain he preferred. That point had been made with a vengeance that morning.

She had driven Lettice to one of her charity meetings. Six women who had been debs with her years before had swarmed around her grandmother, all of them impeccably dressed and asking questions about James, questions that clearly showed a knowledge of him and his habits. Next to their Mazzeo dresses and Adolfo hats, her K-mart jeans had seemed downright grungy, and she had caught herself trying to smooth down her hair. Their disparaging looks had only made her feel more out of place.

She had realized yet again that she was the kind of woman he'd want, but not the kind he *really* wanted. That added humiliation was no doubt a contributor to the current awkwardness between them.

She had noticed that the cooler their meetings grew, the friendlier he became with her son. She'd seen them talking together several times over the last few days. She couldn't help feeling that she was somehow being betrayed. And then she couldn't help feeling silly.

Still, whatever she felt, she wished she could maintain a professional demeanor with the man. But to her disgust, her social clumsiness even seeped into that. She didn't know who was to blame for their coolness. She didn't know if she wanted to know either. All she knew was it seemed to be escalating, and it hurt.

She no sooner stepped into the stallion barn, when she saw James lounging on several bales of hay. She froze in mid-stride, wondering wildly how she could have seen him heading for his car. Maybe he hadn't been headed for his car, just the house. Maybe she was about as dumb as they came.

He straightened with a grace that left her struggling for air.

"Hello," he said.

She swallowed. "Hello."

Nothing more was said, and the silence grew tense and awkward.

The clatter of hooves on concrete brought her back to the present. At the other end of the barn,

Battle Cry was clipped to one of the barn posts and Mac was currying him. Both barn entrances were open to the sun, and it was easy to see that the horse's dark red hide gleamed with health and tender loving care. Anne smiled in genuine pleasure, grateful for the distraction from James.

She walked over and ran her hand down the animal's neck in an affectionate gesture. The powerful muscles bunched and flexed under her touch. Battle Cry accepted the stroking, then moved restlessly away. In fact, she noticed, he was unusually alert and in constant movement. Generally, race horses kept their heads down, showing no interest in their surroundings. It was an irony of nature that the fastest horses always looked exhausted off the racetrack. Battle Cry was an exception, though. He was always pumped up.

A thought she couldn't identify niggled at the back of her mind, but a sixth sense warned her that James had moved up behind her. She tensed, then forced herself to relax. She would just have to ignore him. Still, sensing his gaze boring into her back, she had a feeling she'd be more successful ignoring a hurricane.

"He looks wonderful," she said to Mac.

"Yeah." Mac's hands swept the brushes across the coat with deft movements. He glanced over at James, then back to her, and tapped the large head collar around Battle Cry's neck. "This thing, though, is an annoyance, miss."

"I know, but it's a rule I demand be followed with all the horses." James was so damned deadly silent, she thought, standing off to one side and watching her. She was oddly nervous, as if being scrutinized by a hungry tiger, and she rambled on with her explanation to Mac. "With so many mares coming and going, we really can't get to know them as well as we would like, and the horse collars with the name plates are essential. The last thing we need is confusion over who's who. I carry it through with the stallions because sometimes the men here need to help out in the mares' stables. The consequences could be disastrous if anyone forgot to put on a horse's head collar from lack of habit, or worse, put it on the wrong horse."

"Bet that's happened a few times," Mac said with a chuckle.

"Not here," she said firmly, heat covering her cheeks. She wished he'd never mentioned such a thing in front of James. "Don't even think it, Mac. The last thing a breeding farm needs is to mate the wrong horse to the wrong horse."

Mac smiled knowingly, but it was a thought she refused even to consider. No breeder did.

"I'm going now, Mac," James suddenly said.

"Good-bye, sir," Mac said. "Our boy appreciates your visits."

James nodded, then turned to her. "I want to talk to you," he said in a low voice, "about what happened the other night."

Embarrassment heated her cheeks, and she could see Mac cocking his head to listen. She couldn't believe James would bring the kiss up in front of Mac. And she couldn't believe how much she wanted James to kiss her again. "No," she said bluntly.

"Right," he snapped. He spun on his heel and stalked out of the barn. "Good evening, Anne."

She refused to run after him and give herself away—especially in front of Mac. To cover any awkwardness, she smiled and shrugged at the little man, then asked if he wanted the large comb for the mane.

A few minutes later a voice called out behind her, "There you are, Anne."

Anne turned around in time to see Lettice step into the barn. She should have looked out of place in her pearls and pumps, but she didn't. Tibbs was right at her heels. The dog had quickly become Lettice's shadow until even Philip had trouble luring him away. Battle Cry gave the newcomer a cursory look, then turned back to Mac's attentions. He was obviously used to all the various animals and people in his new life.

"Grandmother, I thought you were at one of your meetings," Anne said, frowning. Her grandmother never came out to the barns.

"I've been to two today." Lettice put her hands on her hips and glared at her granddaughter. "I just asked James to stay for dinner and he refused. Why is that?"

Anne wished Lettice had brought this up in private. Or not brought it up at all. Her biorhythms must be in the pits. She shrugged, refusing to be baited. "Maybe he was busy tonight."

"In a pig's eye. What's going on between you two?"

"Nothing," Anne muttered. "Absolutely nothing."

Lettice was silent, and Anne realized she might have given away more than she meant. Quickly she added, "Nothing is wrong, if that's what you mean, Grandmother. I've told you before your imagination exceeds reality. It's business between James and me."

"So you say."

Wonderful, Anne thought. Just what her grandmother needed, more ammunition. Now Lettice would be after her day *and* night on the subject of James Farraday.

Fortunately, her grandmother's attention was drawn to the horse looming in back of Anne. "Is that him? This . . . War Cry everyone here is so excited about?"

"Battle Cry." Anne chuckled at the human snort of indignation behind her. "Yes, it is."

Lettice walked past her to the horse. Only her grandmother would have ignored for days the most well-known horse since Man o' War, Anne thought. Until now she hadn't bothered to come out to see Battle Cry. And it was nosiness, not horses, that had brought her this time.

"Is he friendly?" Lettice asked.

"Oh, yes, dear lady," Mac said. "My boy's the friendliest horse in any stable."

"Grandmother, this is Oliver MacGinley," Anne said. "Mac, my grandmother, Lettice Kitteridge."

"You cannot be young Miss Anne's grandmother," Mac said, sketching a bow. "You're much too young and beautiful yourself."

Anne smothered her laughter as Lettice gave Mac the regal nod. Lettice stretched out her hand toward the horse and said, "May I?"

"Of course, dear lady, of course."

Lettice petted the horse's nose. Battle Cry wickered and butted her hand for more. Another sucker for Lettice, Anne thought.

"He's wonderful," Lettice murmured.

Mac smiled with pride. "The best horse since his great relation, Man o' War. Better, I like to think."

Lettice nodded gravely, then turned to her granddaughter. "Are you coming up to the house for dinner tonight?"

"Yes." Anne glanced at her watch and saw it was almost time for the meal. Tonight was safe enough to join the family. They were one guest shy, thank goodness.

"Good," Lettice said. "Then you can walk back with me. I'm an old woman and I might slip and fall."

"And Roseanne Barr is a size five," Anne muttered.

"I beg your pardon?"

"I'll be glad to walk back with you." Anne knew she was being manipulated, but it would be silly to walk back separately. And Lettice would never let her forget it.

After they left the barn to Mac's flowery farewell, Lettice said, "I don't like him."

"Who? Mac?"

She nodded. "Yes. He's too . . . ingratiating. How can you put up with him?"

"I have to," Anne said, gritting her teeth. "He's James's employee, remember? Anyway, he's just a sweet old man who loves that horse so much he'd do anything to be with him. Including fawning a little. I'm sure he's just trying to be liked."

"That doesn't make him likable in my book. Just devious. It makes me wonder what's behind that humble facade."

"You don't understand, Grandmother. It's tough when you get attached to the animals. They become . . . they *are* your family." Anne sighed, thinking of Digby, her retired gelding. She had so loved riding that horse in races that she'd bought him when he was retired. At least she had been lucky enough to be able to afford him. Not all those who loved an animal could—witness Mac. "To have a horse like Battle Cry under your care is . . . well, it's the pleasure and pride of a lifetime. Mac has no family other than that horse."

"He is a beautiful creature," Lettice agreed.

Anne grinned. Lettice had succumbed to Battle Cry's spell—just as her granddaughter was succumbing to the owner's spell. Her mirth faded at the thought.

"Maybe you're right about James being too busy to stay this evening," Lettice mused aloud. "I think I'll ask him to dinner for another night. I bought a pasta maker on the way home. I noticed you didn't have one."

Anne turned and gaped at her grandmother. Considering the way James had stared at her in the stallion barn, and the flood of heat that swept through her whenever she remembered that kiss, she knew she wouldn't survive sitting across the dinner table from him. "In a pig's eye!"

Lettice smiled. "No, dear. That wouldn't be appetizing."

"I mean James coming to dinner."

"Ahh," Lettice said, looking like the cat who swallowed the canary. "But it would be only a *business* dinner between you two. Right?"

Anne pressed her lips together. "Right."

"I didn't think there would be a problem."

Lettice actually giggled. Anne shoved her hands into her pockets and walked ahead of her grandmother, cursing under her breath. She'd been caught in her own trap, like a mouse between a cat's paws. Thanks to Lettice.

Leaning back against a fence the next morning, James watched Anne walking along the path between the foaling stable and the stallion barn. Busy consulting the clipboard she held, she hadn't noticed him yet, and he took the time to indulge in his favorite occupation. Anne-Watching.

To his disappointment, he couldn't quite see the face that haunted him night and day. His gaze was drawn to her long legs instead. They were slender and firm from her years of riding. Images flashed through his mind of those legs wrapped around his body as she moved in passion with him. His imagination was so vivid, he could feel the silkiness of her flesh surrounding him. It would be perfection.

James closed his eyes for a moment. Lord, but he wanted her. The pent-up need had grown nearly uncontrollable since he had kissed her. He wished things could be different between them, but they couldn't. Still, they couldn't go on like this, so awkward with each other and barely talking.

He opened his eyes in time to see her catch sight of him. She hesitated, then continued. He pushed away from the fence and started toward her. His gaffe in the stallion barn the day before was still fresh in his mind. He knew he had picked the wrong time and place to attempt to talk to her. But they had to talk.

"Good morning, James," she said in the politest of voices when he reached her.

"Anne." He steeled himself to go on. "I owe you an apology for yesterday. It wasn't the time or place for a discussion."

Color tinged her cheeks, and he realized he had used those same words about the kiss.

"I mean in front of Mac," he added in a rush. "But this coolness between us is no good, and I'd like to get things settled with you. Please."

"That's a good idea," she said, tucking her clipboard against her chest. She smiled wryly. "We do have a business relationship—"

"Exactly," he broke in, relieved that she understood. Hell, he was damn grateful she was even talking. "I think we both have to get past what happened the other night if we're going to work together. I'm sure you agree."

The words had no sooner left his mouth than he set his jaw, wishing he could call them back. The last thing he wanted was to "get past" their kiss, but he had no choice. After all these years of guarding his secret, he couldn't risk any more intimacy with her. Could he?

"Oh, I agree," she said. "Believe me, I agree."

He looked at her thick silky hair, the alluring column of her neck, the curving fullness of her breasts he knew was hidden behind the clipboard . . . all denied to him.

The world dimmed. He stepped closer, his hands reaching out to pull her close.

She moved back. To his surprise, she looked almost shocked. Dammit, he knew he had to control his reaction to her, but she didn't have to act so repulsed.

"Is that it?" she asked, her voice cold.

He sensed he was making everything worse, yet he had no idea why. He only wanted their relationship to go back to the way it was before. Well, that wasn't exactly what he wanted, he acknowledged, but what had to be. He needed to reassure her, even if he condemned himself with the same words. "The kiss . . . was a slip on my part. Believe me, it won't happen again. You don't have to worry."

"Well, that makes me a very happy woman, James," she said in a tone that could only be called sarcastic.

"What the hell do you want from me?" he asked, exasperated that she was being so stubborn about accepting his apology.

"Just what I always get. Nothing." She glared at him. "Don't worry, though, I have received your message loud and clear. You want to forget that we kissed each other and remember that we have only a business relationship, and *believe me*, that's all I want too. Happy now?"

She stalked away before he could say another word.

"Oh, yeah, I'm thrilled," he muttered, jamming his hands into his jacket pockets and stalking off in the opposite direction.

Nothing was better. Instead, everything was worse.

That evening Anne hid behind the newspaper as Lettice dialed James's number on the family room telephone. There was an unexpected and unwelcomed reprieve.

"He's making an emergency business trip," Lettice said after she hung up.

Relief and disappointment flooded Anne as she looked up and said, "Oh?"

"Yes." Lettice sat down on the couch. "He said something about a gambling resort deal falling through in the Caymans. He has to go and catch it before it does."

"If he's got to go, he's got to go," Anne said, disappearing back behind the safety of the obituaries. Her brain tried to sort out the information while pain shot through her heart.

"That's in the Caribbean, right?" Philip asked without glancing away from his Nintendo game. "Where Grandpa and Grandma took me to study the turtles last summer."

"That's right," Lettice said. "My son, your grandfather, would be happy to know that you remembered, Philip."

"He and Grandma'd probably shoot me if I didn't. They have that magazine all about the world. They went to . . . Boraxo—"

"Boreno," Lettice corrected him.

"Right, Boreno. And . . ."

As Anne listened to the conversation, images of palm trees swaying in the evening breeze, a moondrenched island beach, and a couple embracing passionately in foaming surf ran through her mind. Unfortunately, she wasn't the female in the picture. She pushed the visions away and set her jaw. If James was on a business trip, that certainly wasn't her business. And if it wasn't *all* business . . .

She bet the farm it wasn't all business. She bet he took one of those silly, fluttery, overage debs with him. Or he'd find some silly, fluttery, overage deb when he got there. All he had to do was smile his famous Farraday smile and crook his finger. And then he'd kiss the life out of them too. And more.

Logic surfaced from somewhere and pointed out that she was being unfair to him. No matter what sort of image she'd conjured up out of her pain and rejection when she was seventeen, she had never seen him act like a stereotypical playboy. She was jealous and she had no right to be. He was going hundreds of miles away, and the thought of not seeing him hurt, oddly. Still, how many times would she emotionally expose herself to him before she learned her lesson? Twice, she sternly told herself. Once when she'd been seventeen, and once the other night. She had other responsibilities now—like Philip. She wouldn't be exposing just her feelings in a relationship. She would be exposing him. His emotional well-being was more important than her own.

And yet she didn't want James to go. She wanted him here, where she could see him, feel his presence, touch him if possible . . .

"Anne."

"What?" she exclaimed, ripping the paper apart at the seams in unconscious frustration. She stared at the two halves, shocked at her action.

"Never mind," Lettice said, smiling.

Anne had a feeling she wasn't fooling her grandmother.

The next morning she felt as if the only person being fooled was herself. She watched from the portico in disbelief as James's car pulled up in front of the house.

"I thought you had an emergency business trip," she said the moment he got out of the car. She noted the passenger seat was empty.

He looked at her for a long moment, making her feel foolish for blurting out the first thing that came into her head.

"I'm on my way to the airport now," he said, carefully removing his sunglasses. "I wanted to check on Battle Cry, see if there was anything you needed from me, a signature on something . . ."

Confusion swept through her. She wouldn't have expected him to be so thoughtful and concerned. "I see."

He reached back into the car and pulled out a bouquet of flowers. "Also, I wanted to deliver these to you . . . and Lettice . . . as my apology for not being able to come to dinner."

He stepped up onto the portico, and she was instantly aware of her heart beating dangerously fast. His smile was boyish and unsure as he gave her the flowers. She could feel the heat of his hand as it almost touched hers. That hand had caressed her, had cupped . . .

White-hot fire flowed through her. He stepped closer. So close, she could nearly feel his chest against her breasts. He stared at her, then lowered his head . . .

"Thank you," she said, gathering the inhuman strength to step back out of reach. Her voice was faint to her ears.

He looked away. "Well, I'll go on up to the barn. I—" He shrugged. "I just wanted to say good-bye."

Without another word he stepped off the portico and disappeared around the side of the house.

Anne stared after him, her fingers stroking the soft petals of a rose.

Days later, Anne had stopped fooling herself. Her morning ride with Digby was fast and furious, an attempt to pound away her growing bewilderment over James.

She missed him. She wanted him. He was more and more a man, not some slick image she had clung to for years. All the things she was learning about him—his love of horses, his caring for a lonely old man, his interest in a lonely young boy—made him real and human.

The flowers he had given her that strange morning had wilted and died, but something inside her was growing, trying to force its way to the surface . . .

She directed Digby toward the stallion barn. As she got closer, she caught sight of Curtis, her stallion foreman, waving frantically at her. Something was up.

Frowning, she rode in.

It was yet another opulent suite in yet another hotel, and he was disgusted with all of them.

James set aside the paperwork, knowing he was too tired and would need to recheck the figure projections later. He leaned his head back on the white sofa and closed his eyes.

Two weeks ago a slight hitch had developed in the negotiations between the current owners of a gambling resort in the Caymans and the cartel he'd put together to buy them out. Their respective lawyers could have easily worked it out, but he'd latched onto it like a hungry shark and taken the first plane out of Philadelphia. And he'd been on the road ever since, visiting all his current and prospective ventures, and drumming up more investors for more cartels. He thought he was in Idaho now, but he couldn't be sure. The days had blurred into jumbo jets and conference rooms. He did know the paperwork he'd just been reading involved a ski resort somewhere in the Rockies.

A wry smile touched his lips. Business was in great shape, but he wasn't. Being latitudes and weeks away from Anne was hardly the cure he'd hoped for. His sleepless nights in his damned empty bed attested to that. There was no denying he wanted her more than ever. She'd been an ideal once. Now she was an obsession. Being away from her hadn't suppressed the urges to act on that obsession. If anything, they were worse, disrupting him at every turn. So far he had resisted the urge to call and see about Battle Cry. He was sure the horse was enjoying his retirement with great enthusiasm. Truthfully, though, the last thing he wanted to do was talk about sex, even horse sex, with Anne. That was a torture he wouldn't survive.

One of the notions that had started going around and around in his head surfaced again. He frowned, wondering if he really ought to examine it. Ignoring it wasn't giving him any peace.

Could it be that he was still being victimized by his past years of low self-esteem? Most dyslexics did suffer that, he knew. It might be he wasn't giving Anne enough credit. She had never shown signs of snobbery, social or physical. She had a son who wore a hearing aid. Philip was a good kid, well-adjusted and responsible, and Anne was a big factor in his shaping. If she wasn't supportive, it would show in the boy, he was sure. Would that support transfer to an adult?

He rocked his head from side to side. He didn't know. He didn't know if he was crazy. He didn't know if he could take a chance. He was too old to ride an emotional whirlwind to a bitter ending. He doubted he would ever be prepared for that. He felt so tired, weary of fighting his impulses, fighting himself.

And yet he wondered . . .

The telephone rang, startling him. He sat up and rubbed his eyes. The room seemed darker than before. He glanced at his watch and realized that somewhere in the midst of his thoughts he'd actually dozed off.

"Maybe I ought to take that as a sign," he muttered, reaching for the phone. "Hello?"

"You better stop traipsing all over the place, young man, and get yourself home."

The imperious tone was suspiciously familiar, and James asked, "Lettice? Is that you?"

"It's not the Queen of England," Lettice snapped. "It took me four hours to track you down there in Idaho."

"What's wrong?" he demanded, her words about his having to come home finally penetrating his brain.

"Battle Cry. There's something wrong with him. Anne needs your help."

Everything clicked into place for him at the thought of her needing him. Why she was an obsession, why he would never be able to accept a rejection from her, why he had never been able to truly excise her from his mind. Why he *needed* her so badly. He was in love with her! And now she needed him—for help with the horse. The idea of a problem with that beautiful gift of nature made his stomach churn. Whatever it was, he'd see it through no matter the time or cost. He'd see it through with Anne. And maybe when that was resolved she'd need him for other reasons. Maybe it was time to stop avoiding the problem of Annie Kitteridge and face her head on.

"I'm on my way."

He slammed the receiver down before Lettice could say another word.

Seven

"All right, bring her in. Steady now."

Anne stood by the entrance of the breeding shed as the men, using calm movements and gentle voices, urged the mare into the stable. With her all-brown coat and black mane and tail, she looked like fifty others at the farm. But she was different, very different.

Curtis came out of the small barn. "Jezebel's Pride is ready. I'm going over now for Battle Cry."

"Fine," Anne replied through gritted teeth. Her stomach was already a knot of anxiety.

"It's probably a wasted effort," Curtis said gloomily. "His first seven mares didn't take—"

"Do it."

He nodded and walked toward the stallion barn.

Anne turned and stared inside the breeding shed. It was ironic that she had seen horses mating on only two occasions, and they had been by accident. The breeding crew were all men, and she had made it clear from the beginning that she would not make them uncomfortable by helping with the actual mating. She had earned their respect with that action. She allowed herself a brief smile. Truthfully, as the only female in the proceedings baring the mare, she would be just as uncomfortable as they.

But this time she had good reason to stay, and the man moving quietly around the shed knew it. A problem had shown up with Battle Cry. A disaster. The farm's reputation was riding on that horse. Her belly lurched ominously at the thought.

Anne focused on Jezebel's Pride. Having been one of the farm's original mares, Jezzy was an old hand at this. She was already munching on the contents of the hay crib. Dr. Adamson, the veterinarian Anne used, sat on several bales of hay, a much more clinical witness to the spectacle about to take place. She was hoping against hope that they were all doing something wrong and the doctor would spot it. A simple explanation for why every one of Battle Cry's mares was *not* pregnant was hardly likely, but still . . .

She had to get this solved as quickly and as quietly as possible. Although she'd admonished all her people not to talk about the problem, she was terrified it would get out. She'd been over the paperwork, and Battle Cry's initial fertility tests showed a horse with the "right stuff." He hadn't refused one mare so far, so why he couldn't perform . . . ? She groaned, thinking of James. She didn't want to tell him. And the way things had been left between them, she was now feeling more of a failure than ever. She hadn't been able even to take good care of his horse!

The clatter of hooves drew her attention, and she turned back around. Battle Cry literally gleamed with health. Sick at heart, she watched the horse prancing and whinnying in eagerness, clearly scenting the mare nearby. He fought the rope clipped to his head collar, but Curtis was too experienced to allow a randy horse to run amok.

Anne followed the horse until she stood just inside the shed's entrance. Battle Cry was brought to Jezebel's Pride, and the next minutes were filled with a savage splendor and tender domination that only nature could create. In the aftermath Battle Cry stood sweating and shaking, while Jezzy calmly went back to munching hay.

"Well, that wasn't it," Anne muttered to herself, feeling as shaken as the stallion.

The animal had acquitted himself admirably. In fact, as she'd watched his vigorous thrusting, she had found herself wondering about his owner. Would James treat a woman with overwhelming passion and gentleness? Would he move so deftly inside her? Would the human version with him exceed the equine's?

Anne pushed away the lingering sensations she had experienced while watching the animals. James had bluntly told her there would never be a time or place. She ought to be worrying instead about his horse.

"All his reactions are quite normal," Dr. Adamson said, coming up to her after his examination.

She nodded. There was nothing she could say.

They began to walk back to the house as he added, "In fact, that was a textbook case of mating if I ever saw one. And I've seen a few in my time. At least there's no sign of sexual dysfunction . . ."

Anne listened as the doctor droned on about Battle Cry's performance. So much for her prayer that the stallion was as green as a newborn foal on the subject of sex. Unfortunately, he'd caught on early. Probably the same as his owner, she thought with silent sarcasm.

". . . and I sent the samples you gave me to the lab the other day. We ought to have the initial fertility testing results back anytime." He shrugged. "Although it's unlikely, it is possible his original test results are inaccurate. It's more probable that whatever's wrong is subtle. Don't worry, Anne, we'll get it fixed."

She sighed. "If it's fixable."

He patted her shoulder in commiseration. "Have you told his owner?"

"Not yet. I want to be able to tell him exactly what's wrong when I do."

"Smart thinking. It could be anything, even the change in environment that's affecting him. No sense upsetting . . ."

"Mr. Farraday," she supplied when the doctor paused.

"Mr. Farraday before you have to."

Good advice, Anne thought. But when they came in sight of the house she realized the doctor's advice was a moot point. James's car was parked in the driveway.

"I better get moving on," Dr. Adamson said. "I have to go over to the Radissons' place. They have a horse with a hot hoof that refuses to heal."

Anne nodded. She supposed she ought to face James alone. It was a punishment she deserved. Her motives for taking Battle Cry hadn't been as pure as the driven snow. That snow had had a lot of dirt behind it, and she knew it. Her attempted trick with Lollipop's Rainbow was now coming home to roost—with an ironic vengeance.

After seeing the doctor off, she trudged up the

portico steps and into the house. She hung her jacket on the coatrack and slipped off her boots, leaving them on the rubber mat by the front door. Voices were coming from the living room, and she took a deep breath before pulling open the old-fashioned oak double doors. Lettice was seated on the sofa while James was standing by the tall, narrow window.

"Look who's back, dear," Lettice said with a knowing smile. "I was just telling James how much *we* missed him."

"Thank you, Grandmother," Anne said, keeping her gaze on the older woman. Her one look at James, in his chambray shirt and pleated wool trousers, had caused her blood to throb in her veins. "Will you excuse us? I need to talk to James alone in my office."

The room went quiet, a little too quiet. In the frozen silence Anne realized that this wasn't just a social call on James's part. He knew. And Lettice was her number-one suspect on the blabbermouth list of the month.

James strode briskly across the room and out into the hallway without a word. He didn't look at her as he passed. She wished a hole would open in the floor and blessedly swallow her into oblivion. Anything was better than this.

"Thanks a lot, Grandmother," she whispered fiercely.

"Well, you were sitting on your fanny *not* calling him," Lettice snapped back. "I had—"

Anne closed the doors on the rest of Lettice's words. Something about the room bothered her, as if there were one too many tables. But the notion was silly; she knew how many tables she owned. Probably it was nerves. She put the "extra" table question out of her mind and tried to gather the right words to deal with James. None came.

When she reached her office, she found him standing by her bookshelves, looking at the titles. The books were a mix of breeders' information, classics, cookbooks, horror, mystery, and romances. She lifted her chin. She liked what she liked and she wouldn't apologize for it. She just wished he hadn't seen the romances. They revealed a little more about herself than she wanted him to know.

He set her copy of a recent best seller back on the shelf and turned to her. "What's wrong with my horse?"

At least the man didn't dither, she thought. She walked behind her cherrywood desk, seeking protection. Gathering calm words, she said, "He's not . . . performing the way we all hoped, James."

"Is he gay?"

She blinked.

"He is, isn't he?" He paced the room. "It figures. I buy the biggest horse in five decades, and the damn thing would rather have a purse and high heels—"

"No! No!" Anne started giggling. She couldn't help it, with the vision he was creating. "Horses don't have homosexual tendencies. Battle Cry is not gay." She remembered the breeding shed. "Definitely not gay."

"Then what is he?"

James's green eyes were practically boring into hers. His jaw was tight with frustration, and his smile was nonexistent. He looked sexier than ever. The topic of conversation was having its usual effect, and her thighs were tightening slowly with the pull of attraction. Her skin was sensitized, almost irritated with the weight of her clothes. It wasn't fair that he could elicit this kind of response from her—especially when she needed all her wits about her.

She cleared her throat and tried to bring herself under control. "He's . . . well, none of the first mares he's been with have become pregnant. They've all gone back into season again. I told you before, it's not unusual for one or two not to take. But every one so far . . . that just doesn't happen unless there's a fertility problem."

James looked stricken. "You mean he's shooting blanks!"

Anne found herself giggling nervously again. She also nodded in agreement.

"But that's impossible!" he exclaimed, staring at her. "He's been tested, and he came out fine."

"I know. It's practically impossible for his original tests to be wrong, but I'm having him retested just the same. I've had him examined by our vet, and he's in good general health. The vet feels, and so do I, that the sterility is temporary. Just the change in environment can affect a horse. If these tests come back fine, then we'll have more subtle testing done as an added precaution." She looked down at the cluttered desktop. "I'm sorry, James. This is my fault—"

"Your fault?"

Glancing up for a moment, she nodded. "Yes. I should have allowed more time for his adjustment."

"Anne." He came over to the desk. "I was here every day, remember? That horse was as happy in your pastures as Lettice is with a new charity. I saw that myself."

She took a deep breath. "Our breeding schedule might be too . . . vigorous for him. After all, he's unproven—"

"Bull." He began pacing again. "I saw that schedule, remember? I might be inexperienced about breeding techniques, but even I could see you were giving him enough time to recover his potency between matings."

She refused to blush at his bluntness. It was about time she acted like a mature adult around him. Having made that decision, she knew she had to confess her attempted finagling with Battle Cry. James should know she had been ready to pull a dirty trick with Lollipop's Rainbow. He should know just how much integrity she lacked. She owed him that.

"You know the saying 'what goes around, comes around'?" she asked.

"Yes, but what—"

"I . . . I was greedy with him, James."

Her voice caught, and she cleared her throat again to cover it. To her horror, tears she couldn't control trickled down her cheeks. She whipped around so her back was to him.

"Greedy?"

He walked up behind her. She moved away to the window, knowing she'd never calm herself unless she put distance between them.

"I had planned to breed him to Lollipop and tell you after the fact."

"But you did tell me," he said. "When I took the tour that morning. We talked about the custom of the breeder getting a place instead of charging a fee, and you got a place."

"I lied about that!" she exclaimed, her voice shaking with her frustration.

"You mean it's not customary?"

"It's just one of the ways a breeder and horse owner can cover costs. But it's not a hard and fast custom!"

"It sounds like a good deal to me." Chuckling, he approached her again. "Why shouldn't the breeder share in the profits? She's doing all the work and taking as much of a risk with her reputation as the owner is with his money."

She turned to face him, not caring that he was so close. She was determined to get everything out in the open. "Dammit, James! I tried a dirty trick, and now it's come back on me . . . and on you."

He frowned in puzzlement. "But you just said getting a place is one of the ways of covering costs. As an owner who doesn't have to pay breeders' fees, I think it sounds like a damn good way."

"You don't understand." She sighed. "I thought you were using my farm only as a temporary hideaway for Battle Cry—"

"Why the hell would you think that?" he demanded.

"Because you said so that night at the dance!" she replied, indignant. "You said you hadn't inquired about placing him at the big farms in California or Kentucky, that you didn't want them leaking the news."

"I said I thought of you!" He sliced the air with his hand. "I didn't consider any of them because I wanted to place him with you."

"I . . . " She turned around and sniffled back a second set of threatening tears. "I figured that out eventually. But don't you see, I was going to mate Lollipop without consulting you first because I was angry. That was unethical. And now Battle Cry is . . . It's all my fault."

He uttered a low curse, and she closed her eyes, feeling the condemnation. Then his hand touched her hair, his fingers gently sweeping tendrils back from her face.

"You're crying."

"No, I'm trying to refill the river so we don't have another drought this year," she said sarcastically, her survival defenses surfacing at his touch.

He pulled her to him. She knew she should be fighting his embrace, but it felt good to be held by him. She even admitted that she needed it. He rubbed her back in comfort, and she snuggled closer, her tears trickling off. Her cheek was against his shoulder, and she could hear his heart beating faintly but steadily. His long absence seemed almost unreal now.

James held her tightly, blaming himself for not being there sooner to take some of the burden off her. That stupid business trip had been an exercise in selfishness. He had never seen her cry before, not for anything? But seeing the single track of a teardrop on each cheek nearly broke him.

"I'm sorry, Annie," he whispered. "I wish I'd never bought that damn horse."

She managed a chuckle. "No, you don't."

"No, I don't," he parroted, smiling. It was heartening that she could make a joke. And she was right. He didn't really regret buying Battle Cry; he was only frustrated at the moment.

He realized the former awkwardness between them had vanished, thanks to this problem with Battle Cry. Hell, he was almost grateful for it. Almost. Still, if it wound up Battle Cry had developed a sterility condition, then he'd just swallow his pride and let the horse enjoy a real retirement. He doubted that Battle Cry could generate the same prestige and purses if he were put back into racing. He'd just have to make more deals than Donald Trump to get back his investment.

It was just like Anne, though, to confess a "sin." He had tried hard not to laugh. He doubted she would have appreciated it. He had so many things he needed to say to her, but now she needed comforting. And companionship. It wasn't exactly what he wanted her to feel for him, but it would do very well for a beginning. "You've done a great job with Battle Cry—"

She interrupted him. "Someone else could do much better. If you want to move him to another farm, I'll understand."

"Battle Cry and I are happy right here," he said firmly. "You're a top breeder, Anne, with a top reputation."

"Not for too much longer." The break in her voice was clear.

He held her more tightly and said the words he prayed would come true. "Battle Cry will be fine, you'll see."

She didn't answer, content just to be held. And he was quite willing to accommodate her. Minutes passed, and he wasn't exactly sure when the comfort changed to something different. Maybe it was when she began absently toying with the buttons on his shirt. Maybe it was when she pressed her body more snugly to his.

Whatever, he was all too aware of her breasts teasing his chest, her hips aligned with his. One of his legs was almost trapped between her thighs as he kept himself braced to carry her slight weight. His hands were at her slender waist. All he had to do was smooth his fingers down a few inches and he would be cupping her derriere. It would just take one movement to lift her farther into him.

He told himself this was not the time to indulge primitive urges. Definitely not the time.

She looked up at him, and he was lost the moment he gazed into her blue-green eyes. He took her mouth fiercely, the kiss flaming to open passion in the blink of an eye. Her tongue swirled with his, fencing and teasing, and his blood flamed to a volcanic heat. Her immediate response surprised and delighted him. He lifted her to him, his hips crowding against hers. Her fingers dug into his shoulders almost painfully, not to force him away but to pull him closer. She wanted him just as she had the other night by the breeding shed. He'd be damned before he walked away from her again. Not this time . . .

This time, though, she was the one to break the embrace.

She pulled out of his arms and straightened. "I'm not one of your fluttering women, James, who collapses at your feet the moment you kiss them."

He stared at her. "What fluttering women? What are you talking about?"

"Never mind," she said, waving a hand. "Don't kiss me again, okay?"

"Why not?" he asked, knowing she was attempting to erect walls between them. That was another thing he wouldn't allow to happen again. "Are you going to tell me you don't like it?"

"I like it too well," she said honestly. "That's the problem."

"Not from my side of it."

"James, I have a policy of not involving myself personally with my owners."

"You're about to make an exception."

"No, I'm not. And I have a child's feelings to consider. I won't 'indulge' myself at his expense."

"Anne." He took her arm as she began to walk around him toward the front door.

She shook him off. "I'll call you when I get Battle Cry's test results."

As she left the room, he decided he might have a few more obstacles with her than he'd first thought. Still, the thaw was on. All he needed now was a plan.

He was still staring at the open door when Lettice appeared.

"My granddaughter is stomping through the house again. It's nice to see her back to normal." She smiled when he laughed. "I'm glad you're back, James."

"So am I." He walked over to Lettice and took her arm to escort her from the room. "I suppose I should go see that trouble-making horse of mine."

"Did Anne remember her manners for once and ask you to stay for dinner?"

James grinned. "She was . . . busy."

Lettice's eyebrows rose. "Oh? Doing what?"

"Kissing me."

Lettice smiled, and James realized he had an ally in Anne's grandmother. Somehow that didn't surprise him. He remembered years before their families used to joke about him and Anne. No joke now, he thought.

"Ahh. Then I take it you'll stay for dinner?" Lettice asked.

"Oh, absolutely."

He had a feeling Anne wasn't going to like it. But she better get used to it. He planned to be around a long time.

All he had to do was convince her of that.

•   •   •

Anne wasn't pleased to see him at the dinner table that evening, but he figured it was a major step in the right direction when she didn't get up and walk out.

In fact, she was almost congenial by the time they reached the lemon sponge cake. But the way she glanced at him with such wariness, or the frown that appeared whenever he talked to Philip, told him things wouldn't be as easy as he might hope. And truthfully, he wasn't quite ready to tell her *all* about himself.

Taking things slow seemed to be the best way to deal with Anne. He'd have to control his reaction to her. The thought was depressing. Still, restraint made sense only until they'd worked through these little bumps.

"I have to go out again," she announced, pushing her barely touched dessert away. "I want to che—make sure everything's secure for the night."

Philip nodded, unconcerned, while Lettice frowned at her. James smiled nonchalantly. Anne would have an escort, he decided. A very platonic escort this time, but one just the same.

The telephone rang, and she got up to answer it. To James's surprise, Lettice turned her frown on him. He had no idea what he'd done to displease her, but pushed it out of his mind when he heard Anne say the word *test*. His stomach crawled as he leaned forward in anticipation.

"You're sure?" she asked grimly. "I see. Thank you for calling me directly. I really appreciate it."

She said good-bye and hung up the phone. Her expression was angrier than he had ever seen before.

"What?" he asked. "Did they find the problem with Battle Cry?"

"They found it all right." She was silent for a long moment, as if controlling herself. "It seems someone has been systematically feeding him steroids."

"Steroids?"

She nodded. "They build muscles and give an animal a super-healthy look. They can also make a stallion sterile very quickly. That's one of the side effects. One of the gentler, *temporary* ones."

"I take it steroids are not on the vitamin and feed schedule," James said, anger coursing through him as the implications sank in.

Anne smiled bitterly. "They are not."

Somebody wanted to ruin Battle Cry, he thought. And Anne.

He had no idea why, but he vowed that somebody was going to pay. He'd make sure of it.

Eight

"Somebody's tryin' to ruin my boy. Why? Why?"

Anne almost cringed at Mac's words. They were a lament that had run through her head over and over.

"We don't know why," James said gently.

Anne glanced at James, grateful for his presence this morning. She hadn't been looking forward to telling the old man about the horse. The vet had just left after examining Battle Cry again, and Mac had been asking questions, questions she had to face answering.

Battle Cry's sterility *was* temporary, thank goodness. She was damn glad James wasn't blaming her. Another owner would have, she knew.

" 'Tis a jealousy," Mac said darkly. "There are those who are jealous of a horse like that."

She bristled. "Are you suggesting someone on this farm would do such a thing?"

Mack gave her a blank look, then shook his head. "You've got good people, miss. I've seen that myself. But I should have taken better care of my boy. Everybody's had a carrot or a sugar cube for him. Other owners, their guests, even delivery men. All of them wanted a look-see at him, and I, in my pride, let everybody close."

Guilt assailed her. *She* was the one who should have been more careful with Battle Cry and beefed-up her security measures. But who would bother with a horse put out to stud? It was the fabulous racing purses that attracted sabotage.

She laid her hand on Mac's arm. "This was my fault, not yours—"

"Yes, it is," Mac said, pulling his arm away. "This is a shoddy—"

"That's enough!" James snapped, glaring at his employee.

Mac hung his head. "I'm sorry, Miss Anne. I'm just that upset over my boy."

She forced away any anger toward the man. "I understand, Mac. Believe me, I understand." She turned to look at Battle Cry grazing contentedly in the pasture. "The steroids should leech out of him very quickly, fortunately. But it explains why he's been almost jumping out of his skin lately. I wish I knew how he was getting the drugs."

"If we knew how, then we'd know who," James said.

Anne heard the emphasized pronoun *we*, and both pleasure and resentment ran through her. She couldn't help feeling James was being too nice about this. Her confusion about him was mounting—as was her desire. She was afraid she was already in the throes of a crush. Again.

Returning her attention to the problem of Battle Cry, she said, "Curtis and I have talked it over, and nobody, Mac, is allowed near him, especially to give him treats. Curtis will be the one to mix his feed and bring it to him. No one else. Battle Cry's to stay in the pasture next to the barn, where he's visible at all times. The only owner allowed down here is James. No guests, no delivery men. The other stallions will be brought down to the house should their owners visit. They won't like it, but that's too bad. If anyone asks, say we just want to give Battle Cry some peace to adjust to his new life. I know I'm closing the barn door after the fact, but it's the best I can do. At least it'll keep Battle Cry from getting more steroids."

Mac tipped his head in acknowledgment.

She and James left the barn a few minutes later. They stopped by mutual silent consent at the fence enclosing his horse's pasture. Despite her worries, Anne was all too aware of James's body so close to hers. She felt almost hemmed in. But to move away would look childish, and she refused to be childish.

Instead, she leaned on the top rail and stared at the horse, placid and intent on finding the sweet grasses. That restless energy was fading already. He might not look so vigorous on the outside, but he was growing healthier on the inside.

"I'm sorry, James," she whispered.

"Anybody ever tell you that you blame yourself for everything?" he asked, his smile belying his angry tone. "I told you last night to stop it."

"That doesn't make me feel any better."

"Lord, woman, you want the earth." He grimaced. "How could you have known anyone would try such a thing? Even now, knowing that someone has tried to hurt him, it still doesn't make any sense. What's to be gained from it?"

"Ruin for somebody," she said, then took a deep breath. "Probably me."

She'd said it out loud finally. It had kept her awake the whole night. The only explanation for "why" was that somebody was trying to ruin her farm. Somebody must hate her with a terrifying passion to do such a thing. And she had no idea why.

"No. Not you," James said, covering her hand with his. His touch sent sharp signals pulsing through her body. She couldn't pull her hand away without looking silly yet again. Acting one's age certainly had its drawbacks, she thought in disgust.

Oblivious to the torment his touch created, James said, "I've thought about that since last night when we got the report. It could just as easily be me. I could name a number of people who wouldn't mind seeing me take a bath on that horse. I've been very successful in a cutthroat business. Anyway, I can't imagine you having any enemies. You're much too sexy."

She blushed and ducked her head so he wouldn't see. His words gave her more pleasure than they should. When she had her face under control, she turned back. "Very funny, James. I'll tell Eddie Murphy he's got heavy-duty competition."

"If you don't want to discuss how sexy you are, then just say so," he said, grinning at her.

She pulled her hand away. "I don't want to discuss it."

"Spoilsport."

"Thank you very much."

He eyed her sourly, and she couldn't help chuckling. "Turning back to the topic at hand, then," he said, "the question is who."

"And how," she added, following his lead and turning her mind back to the problem with Battle

Cry. Her body objected strenuously. She ignored it and said, "I can't imagine somebody injecting him with the stuff regularly over several weeks. They would have been seen, surely. And Mac's an old hand. He would have noticed the small welts a needle puncture would leave. That's why I think someone's been feeding the drug to him. We take precautions for burglars and vandals, but that's clearly not enough. I cringe when I think of the visitors and deliveries made every week. It's just that there are so many people who come and go here on legitimate business."

"You've never had any problems before," he reminded her. "So why should you have been worried when there was nothing to worry about? You've secured the stallion barn area."

"Too late," she muttered, feeling overwhelmed again.

"I have a feeling now that this method has been discovered, it won't be used again."

She straightened. "What are you saying? That there will be more?"

"Someone's gone to a lot of trouble here for some reason," he said, his expression thoughtful. "What was done to Battle Cry wasn't a lark, but a very calculated move. I doubt they're going to stop just because we've discovered the game."

She could easily sense the anger in him . . . and an odd hesitation. Immediately, she knew he was about to say something she wasn't going to like.

He did. "I can't help thinking that we were meant to discover this. That worries me . . . about you. I think I should be around more—"

"How much more?" she broke in, her suspicions rising at an alarming rate.

"About twenty-four hours more—"

"Twenty-four hours!" she exclaimed, staring at him. "That's day *and* night!"

"Very good, Anne," he said in a schoolteacher's tone. "You get an A."

"And you get an F if you think you're moving in." The notion sent fear raking through her—fear for how fast she would fall for him if he were around all the time. "I might have a problem, but your moving in is hardly necessary."

"I think it's very necessary." He pointed to Battle Cry. "Somebody who's not very nice is up to mischief around here, Annie. And I think you need some protection—"

"Oh, no, I don't! I have Tibbs—"

"He's too busy getting fussed over by Lettice."

"I have employees."

"And I have a personal stake in this. What are you afraid of, Annie?"

That, she thought. The way he said her name, the way he looked at her. The way he touched her, and the way he *didn't*. She was afraid of all of that.

"I understand your wanting to watch over your horse," she said, picking her way carefully through the mine field he was laying. "But I don't need someone to watch over me."

"Yes, you do—"

"No, I don't. I'm hardly helpless." She refused to look away, keeping her gaze steady on those green eyes that haunted her sleep. "If you want to move Battle Cry, I understand. But under no circumstances are you moving in."

She pushed away from the fence and walked down the path.

James caught up with her. "Anne, be reasonable."

"Oh, I am." She smiled sweetly. "I appreciate

the offer, James. Really I do. Only I must say, Thank you, but no."

"I don't like it," he said grudgingly.

She was tempted to tell him to sit on a tack if he didn't, but she decided to be gracious. "I'll be fine, James. I promise to stick close to Lettice. Between her and Tibbs, the s.o.b. who's doing this doesn't stand a chance."

"Let me hire a security firm," he offered, trying another approach.

"No. I won't have the routine of the farm disrupted." She stopped and faced him. Shoving her hands into her jacket pockets, she added, "James, please. Allow me to handle this."

"At least think about it, Annie."

She frowned. She wasn't being obtuse; she really didn't want the routine of the farm disrupted any further. Still, maybe she should consider outside security. "I'll think about it."

"And if anything else does happen, I move in," he said.

"No. I told you that was hardly necessary."

He gazed at her, his eyes unfathomable. "Anne, I have this need to watch over those I . . . care about."

She turned away and closed her eyes against the emotions knifing through her. Mr. Perfect strikes again, she thought. She knew better than to attribute his offer to anything other than "caring" for an old friend. That was all it was.

"Thank you, James, I appreciate that," she murmured, opening her eyes.

"So you agree?"

"Oh, sure," she replied in a careless tone to get him to drop the subject.

"Good." His smile was dazzling.

What a guy, she thought sarcastically. And that was her problem.

What a guy.

James smiled to himself as he helped Lettice set the table for dinner.

So Anne didn't want him to play twenty-four-hour bodyguard. Although he was disappointed, he had to admit her reaction was promising. She hadn't liked his suggestion one bit. The implications were interesting.

He nearly tripped over Tibbs, who growled a warning at him.

James was tempted to growl back. The damn thing had adopted Lettice, as if she were its long-lost mother. Wherever she was, Tibbs was. Underfoot.

"It's not James's fault that you insist on lying right in the pathway," Lettice told the animal. "Now go lie under the table."

With a dejected look the dog slunk between the chairs, out of sight.

James chuckled, then turned his attention to his second major problem. He was worried over what had happened with Battle Cry. And he was more than worried that there would be another incident. He had a feeling Anne was the target. If somebody wanted to get at him through the horse, they would have simply eliminated the animal altogether. He wanted to protect her. . . .

"I didn't know setting a table could elicit that much of a frown, James," Lettice said.

"I was thinking of something," he said.

"My granddaughter, no doubt."

He laughed, and Lettice smiled.

Anne walked into the dining room just then . . . and stopped cold when she saw him. James found his gaze focusing on her breasts. The small yet full curve of them demanded appreciation. He was more than happy to give it.

"James is staying for dinner," Lettice announced, her voice daring her granddaughter to object.

"So I see." She slowly walked farther into the room. "It's hard to believe you two would be setting the table."

"Snob," Lettice murmured, then added, "so what have you decided to do about James's horse?"

"We're still 'discussing' the matter," James said, still looking at Anne.

Lettice glanced between the two of them. "I see."

"Where's Tibbs?" Anne asked, clearly not wanting to continue their "discussion."

"Under the table, where I told him to go," Lettice replied.

Anne bent down and lifted the lace tablecloth. But instead of calling to the dog, she straightened and stared at the material in her hand.

"This isn't mine," she said. "At least I don't think I have a tablecloth like this."

"Really, Anne, you've been working too hard if you can't remember your own things," Lettice said. "And you're worried about Missile Shout."

"Battle Cry," James and Anne said together.

They looked at each other and laughed. James could feel the emotional foundation strengthening between them. He couldn't rush this. He'd waited a long time for her, longer than he had ever realized. A little more patience on his part and all the walls would crumble.

•　•　•

After dinner Anne loaded the dishwasher, then walked over to the back door and removed her jacket from a peg beside it. James took the jacket from her and held it out for her.

She hesitated for a moment, then slipped her arms in. Her fingers brushed her shoulders lightly, and a hot wave of reaction rushed through her. He lifted his own jacket from the rack and put it on.

"Leaving?" she asked, annoyed with the breathlessness in her voice.

He just smiled in answer and called a good night to Lettice and Philip. Then he curled his lip at Tibbs, who wagged his tail in return.

Anne had to smile. "Come on, Tibbs. Want to go for a walk?"

James groaned. The dog looked to Lettice first, who said "go." Anne curled her lip at her grandmother. "When you go back home, take *five* things with you."

"She doesn't mean it," Philip said to Lettice.

"Don't tempt me," Anne muttered.

She opened the back door. Tibbs raced past her, and she stepped over the threshold. James followed. She walked down the back porch steps. James followed. She walked along the path toward the farm buildings. James followed.

She stopped and whirled around. "Are you following me?"

"Nope."

She turned around again and took two steps. James followed. She looked back. Even in the darkness she could see his grin.

"I thought you weren't following me."

"I'm not." He closed the gap between them and took her arm in a courtly gesture. "I'm escorting you."

Her heart pounded heavily at his touch. He had only to look at her these days, and she responded. His touch sent her right off her personal Richter scale. But she resisted the urge to jerk away. Calmly, she stepped back out of his grip. "I have Tibbs to escort me."

"He's not nearly as protective as I am, believe me."

James took her arm again, effectively trapping her. To pull away once was understandable, twice was blatantly announcing his touch was disturbing. He started walking up the path, and she had no choice but to join him.

"Have you give any thought to what I said about a security service?" he asked.

Relief washed through her at the topic of conversation. She'd love anything that would distract her from her acute awareness of the way his fingers curved around her elbow, the way his body moved. The closeness . . .

"I'm thinking about it," she said, forcing herself under control.

Okay, so he was touching her. A couple of inches of contact through her heavy tweed jacket and sweater was nothing to get excited about. So why the hell was she so excited?

"Somebody means to do some harm," he said.

"I agree somebody's trying to do something." She stared up at the night sky, then at Tibbs, who was sniffing every tuft of grass with doggy concentration. "But whoever did it had to know we'd discover it. It was almost as if they wanted to be discovered. I don't want to panic. I talked with my entire staff today, and we're taking a number of added precautions to keep the animals safe."

She stopped walking. She knew she would have

to tell him what she didn't even want to admit to herself. "James, dammit! Curtis and I have gone over and over how somebody could have fed the steroids to Battle Cry. To create this kind of problem in a horse, the drugs had to be fed into him regularly. Not in one or two big doses, but a little at a time, almost daily, until they built up in his system. No outsiders have been here that often. That means either someone has been sneaking in at night—all the stables will now have somebody there at night, all night. One of my people, one I can trust."

She stared at the pastures. Usually there were horses out there at night—most liked the outdoors except in the worst weather. But there were no graceful shapes in the darkness tonight, or any other night from now on. The reminder was all too poignant.

"You said 'either,' " James prompted.

She swallowed. "I did. The other 'either' is that someone who is here on a daily basis did it. Someone I employ."

She had bristled at Mac's remark that morning. But after a discussion with Curtis and looking over the recent delivery schedule, she had concluded there was a real possibility that the culprit was one of her employees. The thought made her sick.

"I'm sorry, Anne, but the idea had crossed my mind too."

James rubbed her arm in a gesture of sympathy. She didn't even think to stiffen in protest and pull away. Instead, she stepped into his embrace as if it were the most natural thing in the world for her.

It was, she thought as she was enveloped in his strong arms. She felt as if she were under siege by outside forces she couldn't even imagine. She had no idea how to counter them, and save her farm and James from disaster.

She tilted her face up and met his lips with a kiss she couldn't deny. The perfection of it, the sensuality of his mouth on hers, was unmatched. It always had been . . . and it always would be.

She wrapped her arms around him and opened herself to the storm lying in wait just below the surface. Comfort turned to passion. Sympathy to naked emotions. She had been too long on her own, without the simple comfort of support from a man. Not any man, she thought. James. Each day she had tried to resist him. Each day the task had become more impossible. She was being pulled toward him helplessly, as if he held all the strings and could command her to his whim. The kiss contained so much more than simple physical attraction. She sensed that each kiss would bring more, much more.

The thought disturbed the layers of need, rippling through them with doubt and logic. It was enough to bring her back to her senses. Confused, she turned away, out of his embrace. Immediately, humiliation set in at her lack of control.

She was searching for the exact right words to excuse her actions, but he beat her to it. Rubbing her arm again, he said, "Sometimes you shock me, Anne."

He ought to see what she did to herself, she thought. "It was . . ."

"Yes?"

"Never mind," she said primly, continuing her night tour of the grounds.

"I'll let you off the hook," he said, joining her. "This time."

She wouldn't ask, she decided. She didn't want to know what he had in mind for next time. She didn't want to examine what was behind her whirling emotions when it came to James Farraday. She didn't think she'd like the answers.

"We'll do it your way for the moment," he added.

"You mean about the security firm?" she asked. If he meant anything else, she definitely had a problem.

"Yes, the security firm. What did you think?"

"Just that." Her voice cracked, and she cursed under her breath.

"If something else happens, then we do it my way."

"James—"

"No, Anne." His tone held a determination that even her grandmother would have found hard to circumvent.

"*If,*" she conceded.

Nothing else would happen, she decided. Nothing else could.

Nine

The problem with great plans was that they took so damn long to implement.

James shoved his hands into his pockets and admitted that his patience with Anne was running out. He watched Digby canter down the drive, Anne sitting proudly astride the animal. He never thought he'd envy a horse. It was as if he'd opened a Pandora's box when he'd finally acknowledged how he felt about her. All those pent-up urges and emotions were now refusing to stay caged in spite of his best efforts.

He forced his body to calmness as he waited for her to ride into the yard. Unfortunately, he could hardly pull her off the horse and make wild love with her right on the spot. It was bright morning, in the open, and Tibbs, who was sniffing around the bushes, would probably mistake his actions and go for his throat. James grinned reluctantly. It was the thought that counted.

"James, honestly," she said when she was within

speaking distance. "This is the fourth day you've been here at the crack of dawn."

"And it'll be the fourth day that I'm here until after midnight," he said, walking over to help her off the horse. "I agreed not to hire a security service or move in."

She made a face. "We didn't agree to your being around every waking hour."

"That's not my fault," he said, grinning at her. Nothing else had happened, and he hoped his constant presence was a reason.

"Next time I'll negotiate better."

Chuckling, he reached up and steadied her at the waist as she dismounted. It was an automatic gesture, one he hadn't thought about beforehand. If he had, he never would have touched her.

The soft knit of her sweater did nothing to hide her slender curves. His hands seemed made to fit the gentle angle of her hips. The small of her back was enticing, daring him to explore further. Her waist was taut yet supple, and he could feel her breath coming faster.

His own lungs seemed devoid of air. To hell with the dog, he thought as he pulled her to him. Her eyes were wide with bewilderment, then knowledge. She didn't move away from him. He touched her hair, letting the dark tendrils curl around his fingers. To his amazement, she didn't protest, didn't pull away. He lowered his head until her mouth was under his in that unique way that was Anne. Her body touched his, breast to chest, hip to hip, thigh to thigh. His senses were filled with the sweet taste of her. The scent of her perfume, subtle and completely feminine, mingled with the earthy scent of her riding. "Pandora's box" was about to explode.

"Ahem!"

Anne jerked away from James at the loud excla-
mation. She turned around to find Lettice grinning at the two of them. Philip stood next to her,
his mouth open in surprise. She smiled weakly at
the boy.

Lettice nudged Philip. "Who knew your mother
was such a kissy-face."

"Grandmother!" Anne glared at Lettice. "Don't
be so . . ."

"Accurate?" James suggested.

Philip was blushing . . . and giggling. "Boy, Mom,
good thing it was only in front of Grandmother
Lettice. You could really embarrass a guy, ya know."

"You could really embarrass a grandmother,"
Lettice said.

Anne grabbed Digby's reins, muttering to herself. James couldn't hear the words as she walked
toward the stables. He didn't have to; her murder-
ous expression said it all.

"You two cut her a break," he said to Lettice
and Philip when Anne was finally out of sight. He
walked over to them. "I was the one kissing her."

"So I saw," Lettice said, smiling gleefully.

"Does—" Philip stopped, then said with the un-
derstatement of the young, "does this mean you
like my mother?"

James smiled. "Yes. I can't help it. I hope you
don't mind, Philip."

He ducked his head, shy. "I—I don't mind."

"You had better get going, young man, or you'll
miss your bus." Lettice swatted Philip on the backside. "I don't think your mother's in the mood to
drive you today."

"Right." Philip dashed off the portico without a
good-bye.

"He's a special boy, James," Lettice said.

"Yes." He was grinning at the knowledge the boy approved of him.

"He's been very hurt by a father who didn't love him. Or his mother."

"I think it's time they stopped being hurt."

He kept his gaze steady on Lettice. He knew they were talking about his intentions with Anne as much as with Philip's feelings.

After a moment Lettice smiled in satisfaction. "I couldn't agree more. But if you two are going to be kissing like that, you'll need some privacy."

Suspicion swirled ominously through his gut. It was flattering to know that Lettice was pleased with him for her granddaughter. Still, he didn't like her tone. He liked it even less when he heard her next sentence.

"I think I can take care of giving you that privacy."

"No!" The word blurted out of his mouth, but this was no time for good manners. Lettice was beginning to steam-roller. "No, Lettice. This is between Anne and me—"

She patted his cheek. "Don't you worry about a thing, James."

"But, Lettice—"

"I'll be subtle. I have been before, with Ellen and Joe."

He had no idea what she was talking about, but he didn't like it. "Lettice—"

"Nature just needs a little shove in the right direction."

"No, nature doesn't—"

"Let me think on just how to go about this."

"Lettice. Lettice!"

Completely ignoring him, she strolled back into

the house and shut the front door in his face. Cursing, James spun around and stared out over the green pastures striped with white fences.

Just what he needed, he thought. Lettice's "help."

"I am not going to Maida Appleton's for dinner!"

"Oh, yes, you are!"

Anne glared at her grandmother. She absolutely was *not* going to his grandmother's house for dinner, not after the way she had kissed James that morning. She was terrified to be around him now. Her resistance was nonexistent the moment she was in his embrace. Unfortunately, if she said exactly why she didn't want to go to Maida's, Lettice would only push harder.

As if her grandmother hadn't already been pushing during the twenty-minute argument, Anne thought. Some corner of logic filtered through her panic, and she realized she was only fueling her grandmother by continuing to argue. Forcing herself to relax, she said, "Please, Grandmother, I've got five mares in labor, with two more possible before the night is over. I just can't go tonight."

"Are you sure you're not weaseling out because of James?" Lettice asked, eyeing her speculatively.

"That would be childish. I'm not a child." She prayed Lettice never talked to Otis, the foaling manager. The possible birth number for tonight was nowhere near five.

Lettice was silent for a moment. "I must admit you're right. Still, Maida will be disappointed. She's asked the whole family. It's very impromptu. Are you sure you can't get away for a little while?"

Anne shook her head, vowing not to blow it

now be being eager. "I really wish I could, now that I think of how much fun we had at that picnic she gave last summer. But they're going to need every hand in the foaling stable tonight. You and Philip go."

"If you're sure . . ."

"Absolutely." A brilliant idea struck her. "James can even drive you. After all, he'll be going to the dinner. And knowing him, he'll be here up until the time he'd have to go anyway."

"Well . . ."

Anne waited out the silence, hiding her impatience behind a forced smile.

"I suppose it's the only logical solution to transportation," Lettice finally said, then sighed in obvious disappointment.

Anne refused to gloat. She'd outwitted her grandmother, but it was much safer not to let Lettice know she knew she had.

At lunch James was even less pleased when he was informed the dinner party would be one short.

"I'll stay," he immediately said.

"No!" Anne and Lettice exclaimed.

Anne stared at her grandmother, surprised. Lettice had been pushing James at her since . . . since forever. She would have thought . . .

"I mean, how will Philip and I get to Maida's?" Lettice asked, shrugging. "And Anne is going to be up all night delivering horse babies—"

"Foals," Anne corrected her, grinning. Her grandmother was determined not to pick up the language.

Lettice nodded. "She simply can't come, I do see that. And Maida will understand. We'll be out for just a couple of hours, James. Anne will be perfectly fine."

"She's right, James." Anne tried to keep the

triumph out of her voice. The thought of him staying was very tempting. And that made it frightening. "I'll be in the foaling stable the entire time. And things have been quiet—"

"That's what worries me," he said.

"I know." She forced herself to hold his gaze. Looking away might reveal her inner state. "I'm not taking anything lightly, I promise. But I'll be fine. Besides, *your* grandmother would never forgive you if you didn't go."

That seemed to be the turning point of the argument, because Anne found herself blessedly alone by evening. She sighed with relief and sprawled stomach-down on the sofa, indulging herself in some sorely needed inner peace.

"Thank you, Aunt Maida," she whispered, tucking a throw pillow under her cheek.

Tibbs hopped up on the sofa and squeezed between her and the back cushions. Reaching around, she scratched his head. It was nice to have her dog back too.

Lying there, she was all too aware of the tension that had been building inside her. The last few days she had felt as if she were a pressure cooker about to explode. She was on constant nerve-racking alert over Battle Cry. All of them were. Combine those worries with her growing feelings for James, and it was no surprise she was a wreck. The refused dinner invitation had been a release valve, and now she had the evening with no pressure, no cares, no Lettice . . . and no James.

Why, she wondered, was she losing her control with him? A snort of frustration escaped her. What control? The past days he had simply been a presence—a constant presence, a comforting presence, a sensual presence. He had kept his distance until this morning. . . .

She sat up, any thoughts of relaxation long gone. Tibbs gave her a dirty look for the interruption. She knew exactly how the dog felt.

"Damn him, why does he have to be so . . . caring?" she whispered into the darkening living room. Tibbs laid his head on her lap. She petted him absently.

She wished she could keep her image of James, that one of a self-centered playboy who kissed a young girl and threw her away afterward without a word. For years she had lived on that harsh image, unforgiving of one kiss. She wondered now if she had married the first playboy who came along to give herself a dose of reality in case she ever wavered toward James.

"Naaa, marrying Ellis was just plain old stupidity," she muttered, tossing the pillow aside.

Unfortunately, Ellis wasn't her problem. James was. James was a lot more of a problem. And that was the problem.

Anne groaned, holding her head in her hands. She had never felt so confused in her life. James wasn't the James she'd thought he was. James was caring and concerned. He had a sense of honor not much seen in this world. And he was fun. She knew words like *shallow*, *vain*, *narcissistic*, and *conceited* just didn't apply. He had flaws. He was stubborn beyond belief, bossy, and argumentative. And yet he was perfect. And she was coming to love perfect. . . .

She pushed herself off the sofa, refusing to continue the thought. Her mind wasn't ready to accept, not yet. Her heart, however, was more than ready.

As she went into the kitchen, she half wished she'd gone with the others. But she did need this time to herself, even though it was hardly peaceful. By the time she'd pecked through a scant meal, she was more restless than ever. Tibbs, who had followed her, got most of the salad, not his favorite.

She was about to clean up the few dirty dishes when Tibbs lifted his head. The dog slowly rose to his feet as a low growl sounded in the back of his throat. A curl of true fear churned in her stomach at the dog's reaction.

Someone was outside.

But Tibbs did no more, which meant he knew who or what was there. She jumped when the knock came at the back door, then immediately calmed herself. It was probably one of the guys with some problem that required her attention. Maybe she hadn't been fibbing about a large number of foals after all. That would be nice.

Still, she couldn't help wondering if James was right to be so worried. She shook her head and walked to the door. Cloak-and-dagger stuff was for the witching hour, not the Cosby half-hour. She whisked open the door and stared at the visitor on the threshold.

"May I come in?" James asked.

The silence was deafening.

Finally Anne found her voice. "But you're supposed to be at dinner . . . Where's Grandmother and Philip?"

"At dinner," he said. "I . . . well, let's just say I wasn't hungry. May I come in?"

James forced himself to smile nonchalantly. He wasn't sure of his welcome, but he was sure of his purpose. The farther he had driven away from Makefield Meadows, the more he'd known he shouldn't. Lettice's constant speculation on the who and how of Battle Cry's diet of steroids had only strengthened his desire to return to the farm.

"I told you I would be fine," Anne said, aware the fire was surfacing in her.

He shrugged. "I know. I'm being paranoid. It's my life's work from which I cannot be thwarted. May I come in, or do you plan to leave me staring at a door all night?"

After a moment she stepped aside. "I suppose."

"Your enthusiasm overwhelms me," he said, entering the kitchen.

"Take what you can get and be grateful."

He would, he decided. Right now he was grateful she hadn't slammed the door in his face. The feeling of something about to happen hadn't abated now that he was here. His instincts were still on the same track.

"Coffee?" she asked, walking over to the counter.

He nodded, then took off his coat and hung it on one of the rack pegs. "I didn't expect to find you at the house. In fact, I went up to the foaling stable first."

She blushed, then laughed in embarrassment. "Promise you won't tell Grandmother."

"Promise," he said, grinning. And he vowed he'd never tell her about his panic when Otis had told him he hadn't seen her all evening and didn't expect to.

"I hope your grandmother won't mind that I skipped out," Anne said as she filled a mug with coffee. "I needed some time to myself."

"I doubt she'll notice. She'll be too busy thinking up ways to punish me for committing the ultimate sin of rudeness." He sat down. "I showed up, kissed her hello and then kissed her good-bye."

"You *are* in trouble." She sat opposite him and

added, "I'm not sure whose grandmother is worse for propriety, yours or mine."

"Mine," James said, liking the way her hair just brushed her shoulders. And the way her breasts were enhanced by the pale yellow sweater. He forced himself to remember their conversation. "My grandmother always thought Emily Post was an upstart. I could never get away with anything less than 'proper' with her. It seems now like we fought continually over what I should be doing when I was a teenager. But she taught me a sense of rightness and fair play. I love her dearly."

"I—I always thought you were a social goody two-shoes, James."

He laughed. "Hardly. Ask my grandmother."

She looked as if she didn't believe him. He grinned, wondering what she had thought of him all these years. He did attend a lot of high society functions, but because of the potential for investors. He could almost pick and choose his partners, and that was part of his success in putting together profitable syndicates. It was ironic that someone might think he was a social butterfly.

"How will Grandmother and Philip get home?" she asked.

"Don't worry, I didn't leave them to walk. My grandmother's car will bring them."

She nodded. The room became quiet.

"Why did you go to California all those years ago?" he asked.

The air was suddenly charged with a strange tension, and her expression became wary. He hadn't expected that kind of reaction to his question.

"Because," she said, and paused. "Because I wanted to race, and that was where the racing opportunities were."

"Why did you marry that movie producer, Ellis Crawford?" It was a question he had meant never to ask, but it had been a burning one lately. "I'm sorry. It's none of my business."

"You're right, it's not." Her gaze was as no-nonsense as her voice. "But you probably know already, through the grandmothers."

He nodded. He did know something of her marriage through the grapevine. "So why not tell me anyway?"

She snorted, an unladylike sound that didn't detract from the lady she was. "It's no big deal. I was attracted to him because of his interest in horses. He owned several. But what I thought was common ground between us was only a tax shelter for his movie earnings. He seemed so caring at first, but later I learned he just knew how to stroke the emotions and the ego. Actually, that's what makes him a good producer. He knows what to do to smooth over dissension. But he didn't give a damn about anybody but himself. He married me because he thought I made him look good with 'Old Money.' And because marriage kept him 'safe' with his affairs." She ran her finger around the rim of her mug, then shrugged. "I hadn't realized that at the time. And then when Philip's hearing problem was discovered, Ellis decided his own son was an embarrassment for not being . . . perfect. I stayed too long in the marriage. Until it was almost too late for Philip."

She looked so vulnerable. Protective urges rose in him. She was blaming herself too much, not seeing that she had been trying to make a marriage and a family. His Annie was very good at guilt, he thought with silent amusement.

"Philip is well-adjusted, so you didn't stay too

long," he said. "There was no easy solution, but you did the best you could to make a family. That's not a bad thing, Anne."

She cleared her throat. "I hope so."

"I was sorry when I heard you married Crawford. I was sorry you married anybody."

Her eyes widened. "You were . . . sorry?"

"Yes. I was sorry." He smiled. "I think I was in love with you even then."

She looked about as shocked at the words as he felt at saying them. But he'd said them. Finally and at last he'd said them. The tension had transferred to him now as he waited for her reaction. Any reaction—as long as it was the right one.

"I . . . Oh, dammit all, I'm going out to check that everyone's bedded down for the night." She shoved back her chair, grabbed her jacket, and headed outdoors.

Her reaction could have been worse, he decided, feeling slightly deflated as he got up to follow her. And it could have been a hell of a lot better.

Once they were outside, they didn't talk about what he'd said. They didn't talk about anything at first, and then only about horses. Battle Cry, in particular.

They walked next to each other, not touching. He was afraid to touch her. He wanted a response of emotions and commitment, not a purely physical one. That awkwardness he'd felt weeks earlier with her was growing again. He had no control over it, and he couldn't stop it.

Dammit, he thought as they returned to the house. Everything was secure, and not a single villain had jumped out from the bushes to attack them. He was almost ready for that. It beat the heck out of waiting for Anne to say something more than "Dammit all" to his declaration of love. Instead, he was becoming more and more positive that she was trying to think of a nice way to reject him. Half of him wanted to take his words back, and the other half was glad they were out. Bitterly, he admitted at least he wouldn't be rejected for his dyslexia. He hadn't even gotten around to telling her about that.

"Well, everything looks quiet," she said, hanging her jacket on the peg. She kept her back to him.

James decided he'd have one last discussion with her, even if it killed him. He grabbed her arm and spun her around. "Anne, we have to talk . . ."

The words trailed away when he felt the unique sensation of her flesh under his palm, sensed the turmoil inside her, and saw the raw need on her face. His control shattered.

He pulled her into his kiss.

Ten

His mouth was hot and drugging, and her own blossomed instantly at the first touch of his lips. Any thought of resistance was gone. The kiss was like an explosion of every repressed urge she'd ever experienced. He had said the most surprising, the most devastating, and the most confusing things to her tonight. Things she'd never even allowed herself to think of; things she was still afraid to face—and wanted so much. She could resist everything but love.

The kiss, instead of intensifying, gradually softened. The primitive passion was still there, but was fading into the background momentarily. She felt poised on the edge of a precipice. She had heard the words. Now she had to feel the truth of them—just for herself. She was old enough to know the difference between sex and love. Earlier tonight she hadn't wanted to face her feelings for James. Now she knew the time for denial was long over.

James lifted his head. Smiling, he tucked a curl of her hair behind her ear, the gesture loving and sensual in the same moment. "Annie . . ."

"Dammit, James, but I love you," she whispered, then sighed and relaxed against him. "You make me crazy."

He grinned. "You've been making me crazy all of my life."

"Good." She wound her arms around his neck and pressed herself against him.

"As long as you're happy." His voice was oddly breathless. She smiled just before his lips found hers again.

The last of the restraints broke with the security of the second kiss. His hands slipped under her sweater to find her flesh, his strong fingers pulling, tugging . . . cupping. She moaned into his mouth as the blackness closed in on her.

She wasn't thinking any longer. She was desperate only to feel—feel the sensations of his mouth everywhere on her flesh, his muscles under her hands, his hips cradled intimately in hers. She had wanted him for a long time, and she had fought the rightness of it until she'd finally been trapped by it.

Suddenly he pulled away and lifted her into his arms. Dizzy and surprised by the sudden movement, she clutched at his shoulders and opened her eyes. He walked purposefully out of the kitchen.

"What are you doing?" she asked.

"Carrying you up to the bedroom."

She considered the idea. "Okay."

"Anne, we really have to work on your enthusiasm level."

She kissed his jaw, the taste of him better than the finest wine.

"Then again, maybe not," he murmured.

She snuggled against his chest. "Did I ever tell you that you were perfect?"

"No. Am I?"

"Absolutely."

"Forget I said *anything* about your enthusiasm level. It's fine, just fine . . . don't do that when I'm carrying you."

She smiled and undid another button on his shirt. She slipped her fingers inside, threading them through the swath of hair on his chest.

"Go ahead, keep not listening to me," he said, kissing her temple.

He climbed the stairs at a speed that seemed unwise, somehow managing not to step on Tibbs, who was padding alongside them. At the top he stopped and said to the dog, "No! Stay!"

Tibbs sat down and stared at him. Anne smothered a chuckle at James's smile of victory. Then to her surprise, he walked unerringly into her bedroom.

She straightened in his arms. "How did you know?"

"I made it a point to," he said cryptically, kicking the door shut.

He laid her on the bed, coming down on top of her. The long-suppressed passion roared back like a tidal wave, devastating and unstoppable. His mouth was a hot fire, pulling her into its all-consuming heat. Their tongues dueled and mated. Hands worked busily as clothes became encumbering and unnecessary. Her sweater was peeled from her slowly, and he strung kisses across every inch of revealed flesh. Need coursed through her in waves that overwhelmed her sanity. She pushed his shirt away, reveling in the feel of his heated skin.

She was already aching for his touch, and she groaned when his thumb skimmed over one tightening nipple. She twisted beneath him, desperate to feel all of him. She wanted more, but he continued to torture her with kisses that encircled the upper slopes of her breasts.

"James, please," she whispered, guiding his mouth to a diamond-hard point.

His lips enclosed her, branding her flesh like no other had. Her blood was pulsing through her veins as a hot need tightened in her belly. She didn't know if she could survive this tender torment, and she didn't care. She only knew that this was James, and she loved him. She needed him, needed to feel all of him against her . . . inside her.

James tried to hang on to some semblance of control. He had waited so long for this, and he wanted to stretch out every second to an unforgettable crescendo. But she was writhing under him, stroking his back, her fingers digging into his shoulders. Her skin was like silk, compelling a man to touch it in wonder over and over again. And her mouth . . . The sweet flame she created with lips and tongue was enough to send him over the edge. All admonishments of gentleness and finesse flew out of his head. This was Annie, and she was finally his. Need and desire drove him to brand every inch of her, to do it now, before this gift was gone.

The rest of their clothes were shed, and secret places were revealed, stroked, and worshiped. She found the shape of him. He found her heated depths. She took him into the cradle of her hips, their bodies pressing their lengths one against the other. She took him farther, until he was inside her completely, totally, possessing all of her even as she possessed him.

And then it began, the age-old movements of nature that too often meant too little, and this time meant so much. Higher and harder love drove them with its demands, until it shattered with a piercing light, hurling them both into the gentle oblivion.

Reluctantly, Anne surfaced to reality. James's weight was heavy, yet she felt content. His arms were secure around her, holding her in a way that left her breathless and satisfied. She felt giddy and shy, happy and nervous all at the same time. She had no idea where this would now take her, but she knew she had to trust it—trust James. In some ways she had always trusted him. The impossible had happened . . . and she was scared to death it wouldn't last.

He kissed her shoulder and shifted slightly, giving her room to breathe. She sighed, both grateful and disappointed.

"I love you," he mumbled.

She chuckled. "I love you."

He nuzzled the soft column of her throat, the curve of her collarbone, the sensitive hollow just under her ear. . . .

"James." Her voice was faint. "Philip . . . Grandmother . . . They'll be back soon."

He glanced at the clock on her bedside table and groaned. "Damn!"

She laughed and lightly smoothed her hands down his back.

"I have a feeling I'm not going to like stolen moments for long," he said, raising his head.

He knew he should tell her about himself, but something held him back. If this moment were an illusion, he wanted to keep it just a little longer.

In the darkness he sensed more than saw her smile.

"I . . . this is all so new . . . and yet it's not," she said.

"I know." He had never thought of her as shy, yet she was now. Anne would always have unexpected facets to her, facets he would delight in finding. He hadn't meant for this to happen tonight, but he hated the thought of leaving her at this moment. It was the last thing he wanted to do. Feeling her body soft and supple against his was tempting him to steal a few more minutes with her.

"I should go," he said, tracing his finger around one rosy nipple. It tightened instantly.

"Yes."

"I love you, Annie."

"I love you, James." She ran her palms over his shoulders and down his back in an exquisite caress.

He shuddered at her touch and kissed her . . . and kissed her again. . . .

Anne's sleep was slowly and relentlessly penetrated by two things. There was a horse sitting on her chest, squeezing the breath from her. And voices were chattering away, not close but close enough to be annoying.

Then she realized the horse wasn't a horse, but James lying on top of her, and the voices belonged to her grandmother and her son.

Lettice and Philip had arrived home from Maida's

dinner, and James was lying naked in her bed with naked her. The combination was unthinkable.

"Oh my God!" she moaned, pushing and shoving James to wake him up.

"Wha' the . . ." he began in a groggy voice, fighting her hands.

"Shut up!" she said, clamping her fingers over his mouth. He stiffened, then froze with her when the voices outside the room grew louder. In silent fascination they both watched the thin sliver of hallway light that seeped under the bedroom door.

". . . but his car's here, Grandmother Lettice."

"Yes, dear. I did see it." Lettice's voice was stronger and louder than usual. "He's probably with your mother in the foaling stable. Remember how busy she expected to be this evening? I'm sure Mr. Otis is grateful for another pair of hands."

Giggles surfaced from nowhere, and Anne tried desperately to suppress them. This wasn't funny—especially if they were caught. To her horror, James's shoulders began to shake with amusement. The giggles were infectious.

"Well, maybe," Philip said, his voice dubious. Some of the light was blocked from under the doorway. They were right outside. "Maybe we ought to check and see if Mom's sleeping."

Anne fought back a scream of panic. Please, she thought, do Mom a big favor and don't check on her.

"But, Philip, if she were asleep in her room, James's car wouldn't be here. Besides, it's very late. We stayed way past both our bedtimes tonight. I know you're really tired."

Anne could hear her son yawn as if on cue.

"See?" Lettice chided. "You just get yourself right into bed, young man. . . ."

The voices drifted down the hall, and light reappeared fully under the door. James lifted her hand from his mouth as they both relaxed.

"That was close," he whispered, sitting up. He pulled her up next to him, his arm around her bare back. "I'm sorry, I fell asleep."

"It's not your fault, James," she whispered back. "I'll have to sneak you out of the house."

She began to giggle again, like a nervy teenager. She felt like one.

"Shh!" James hushed her. Near silent laughter erupted from him.

"Stop that, or we really will get caught." She was grinning in spite of her words.

"Mmmm." He kissed her cheek. "Good thing Lettice headed Philip off about coming in here. I don't think he's ready for a lesson in the birds and the bees."

Especially one involving his mother, Anne thought, her stomach queasy at the notion. If James were her husband, it would be different. . . .

She stopped herself when she realized what she was considering. She didn't know what the future held, and she wouldn't hurt herself by anticipating it.

They waited in near silence for the sounds of the others to gradually quiet into sleep. James's hands wandered upon occasion, much to Anne's aggravation—and pleasure. Okay, she decided when his thumb lingered on her nipple, slowly rubbing the nub to life. She wasn't perfect, and she was damn glad of it.

Long safe minutes later they were presentable and tiptoeing down the stairs. Tibbs met them at the bottom, a tail-wagging co-conspirator rather than a barking menace. In the dark kitchen she opened the back door, wrapping her satin robe tighter around her against the chilly spring air. Tonight had been inevitable, and yet it all happened so fast. Being with James, hearing him say he loved her, felt like it had happened to someone else. Doubts pushed at her consciousness. She shoved them away, praying this was reality.

"I hate the thought of going," he said, adjusting the mandarin collar under her chin.

She nodded. "This can't happen again, James."

"What do you mean, this can't happen again?" he demanded in a low voice.

His anger was unmistakable, and she quickly added, "I mean here in the house. Not with Philip. I love you, James, but I have to set an example for my son."

"Of course. That wasn't what I meant." He ran his hand through his hair. "I thought you were talking about stopping this cold and not seeing me again."

"It would be like trying to stop a hurricane," she whispered.

"Good." He pulled her against him and kissed her, his mouth rekindling the hot fire. Finally, he lifted his head. "It better be like trying to stop a hurricane. In fact, I'm depending on it."

She didn't understand his words.

"Anne . . ." He let go of her and cleared his throat. "Anne, there's something about me you don't know."

He sounded so ominous, she was almost afraid to find out. "What?"

At first he was silent, which only heightened her anxiety level. Finally he said, "Oh, hell. I'm dyslexic, Anne."

"You're . . . That's a learning disability, right?"

"Yes. I've overcome it . . . except when I'm tired. Then I have a tendency to mix up letters."

"Oh." Relief washed through her. "You made it sound as if you were a mass murderer or something." She gazed at him, frowning. He looked so anxious that she wondered if there was more to confess than a childhood problem. "Is there anything else?"

"You don't seem . . . concerned."

Puzzled, she said, "I didn't mean to sound unconcerned. Of course I'm concerned. It must have been very frustrating when you were a child. I know, I see Philip's frustrations. But it's just that you sounded so . . . I don't know . . . like you were about to tell me something horrible about yourself. Dyslexia isn't horrible; it's a learning disability."

He grinned at her. "Very true. I just didn't know if you knew about it."

"James—"

"Never mind." He kissed her soundly on the lips. "It's getting cold. I'll be here first thing in the morning."

She smiled. For once she would be ecstatically happy to see him first thing in the morning. Then her happiness faded.

"What happened to that smile?" he asked.

"I'd forgotten about Battle Cry and why you were coming so early every day."

"Good." He grinned when she lifted her chin. "A little temporary forgetfulness won't hurt either of us. The worst thing is being vigilant when nothing's happening. Neither of us needs ulcers."

She nodded.

"We'll resolve it one way or another, I promise."

He kissed her again. "Hell, I don't want to go at all."

"I don't want you to."

"But I must . . ."

She nodded, not trusting her voice to give the proper answer.

"We'll have to work on this."

He kissed her one last time and then was gone.

Sighing, Anne shut the door and slowly climbed the stairs. James was quite right. They'd have to work on it.

When she was finally back in bed, she stared at the opposite wall before turning out the night-light. Her thoughts were a jumble of hope and happiness, and she was terrified she'd discover in the morning that this night with James had been a dream.

Something on her bureau drew her attention, and she focused on the set of cloisonné brushes next to her jewelry box. She didn't own a set of cloisonné brushes.

Immediately, she rolled away from the odd sight and turned out the light. She didn't care where the brushes came from, just as long as they were there in the light of day.

Like James.

He was there before she took her daily ride.

James grinned as he watched Anne slip out the front door before seven in the morning. She looked young and innocent with her jeans and denim jacket, her silky dark hair in a French braid. Underneath those ordinary clothes was the temptress only he knew. He got out of the car and quietly shut the door. She smiled at him, and he decided it was about to be a beautiful day.

"Am I too early?" he asked.

"Right on time." She stepped into his arms, and he kissed her.

"I love you."

"I love you," she murmured.

He smiled. A guy could really get used to this.

"Did you sleep?" she asked.

"My bed was lonely. Although if you had been there, I wouldn't have slept at all."

"Sex maniac."

"Only with you."

"Good." She pulled away from him.

He made a face at her. "Annie, you're supposed to throw yourself at me when I profess my fidelity and make sexual innuendos, not walk away."

"I'm saving my attack for later."

"It better be a good one," he muttered.

"Promise." She patted his arm. "Come on, let's make our usual morning rounds, otherwise people might wonder."

"Do you care?" he asked seriously.

"No. And yes." She looked worried. "I—I want to get used to it first . . . and then there's Philip."

"Okay. I understand." He did understand how she felt. He was disappointed, too, that she didn't want to shout it from the rooftops. "Let's go."

The farm was already up and awake, the horses rising with the dawn and the humans following suit. Anne checked in at the mares' stables, then the foaling stable. James said not a word, only grinned, when the foaling manager commented on the quiet night. Anne blushed.

James found it a pleasure and a torture to walk next to her. He would have thought the aware-

ness between them would have been assuaged
with lovemaking. Instead, it had been heightened.
He wanted desperately to love her again, and re-
sented that they couldn't. And doubts, irrational
as they were, were growing. Maybe she didn't want
to. Maybe she was having second thoughts.

Clenching his fists, he realized he'd never been
more unsure of himself than now. Her reaction to
his confession of dyslexia had bothered him in-
creasingly during the night. He had hoped for
acceptance, and she had accepted him. Then why
was he feeling so deflated now?

"You're quiet," she said.

He mentally shook away the disturbing thoughts.
"Just daydreaming. There is a topic I think we
should discuss—the fact that I have this overwhelming urge to drag you into the nearest empty
building."

She glanced away, then looked back with longing in her eyes, and he knew she felt the same
way he did. Contentment ran through him. She
didn't want their separation any more than he
did.

"We'll have to think of how to sneak around all
these obstacles," he said, taking her hand.

She tried to pull her hand away. "James. Philip—"

He squeezed her fingers gently, but refused to
let go. She eventually relaxed.

"I know," he said. "Philip. I promise we'll be"—he
leaned over and whispered—"discreet."

"Oh, brother." But she was laughing. "And what
do you know about being discreet?"

"Not a thing," he said innocently.

She made a face at him.

"The morning fog's burning off," he added,
changing the subject.

"Nice way of avoiding 'discreet,' " she said.

"Thank you." Fenced-in pastures sprawled in either direction as they walked toward the stallion barn. "This place is as beautiful as its owner."

She ducked her head. "Thank you."

The tension, dispelled by the teasing, easy conversation, was returning. Desire clamored inside him, and he fought it back by looking around at the peaceful scene before him. Several horses and foals galloping along the fence in a far meadow caught his attention. He pointed at them. "It's incredible to see magnificent creatures like those enjoying the morning. Funny, one looks a lot like my horse. I didn't know you had another horse that resembled Battle Cry so closely."

Anne stopped dead and uttered a barnyard curse. He stared at her in shock.

"That's because I don't!" she exclaimed. "That *is* Battle Cry! He's in with some mares."

They both started running.

"We can't catch him with our bare hands!" Anne shouted. "Go get help from the barn. I'll try to distract him from—"

"You get help. I'll do the distracting—"

"Dammit, James! I need your help, not an argument!" Before he could say a word, she swerved, then threw herself at a fence, scrambling over it to take a shortcut to the far pasture.

He veered toward the barn, all the while cursing her obtuseness. She had damn well better be all right after he got help, he thought. Because then he was going to kill her.

"Battle Cry's loose!" he yelled the moment he was within hearing distance of the barn. "He's in with some mares in the far pasture!"

Curtis, who had just emerged from the barn,

looked at the nearest pasture, saw it was empty, and began to shout curses and orders. Men ran everywhere at his commands.

"Redman Chief just went crazy in his stall," Curtis said, running up to James, "and we were all in with that! But it was only for a few minutes—"

"I don't give a damn how it happened!" James said over his shoulder as he raced back toward the pasture. "Just hurry. Anne's trying to distract him now."

He left Curtis to his cursing and shouting and returned to the pasture in record time. His heart stopped when he spotted Anne in the middle of the field, running dangerously close to the galloping horses while screaming and waving her jacket. It wasn't worth the risk to herself just to keep the stallion from mating with a few mares not on the schedule.

He boosted himself over the six-foot fence and peeled off his sweater, swirling it above his head and yelling at her, "Get out of there before you get hurt!"

She shook her head. "Got to . . . kept them . . . moving!"

He swore at her, more angry than he ever thought he could l at her foolhardiness. The men arrived with ropes and halters. Not bothering to waste more breath, he ran onto the field, grabbed Anne around the waist, and pulled her back to the fence.

"Dammit, Anne," he said when they reached it, "you could have been hurt, and for what? A couple of foals born on the wrong side of the blanket?"

"And that could ruin my farm," she said. She was gasping for breath, but that didn't stop her from stiffening with indignation. "And the purity of Battle Cry's lineage."

"I don't give a damn about that. I care about you. I love you." He rubbed his forehead, completely winded. "That's it. Our agreement's terminated as of now. A security firm will be here before the day is out."

"But—"

"No buts, Anne. Until we catch whoever is doing this, they'll be here twenty-four hours a day . . . and so will I."

Eleven

"I shouldn't have tried to help with the other horse. . . . I should have been watching my boy. . . ."

Anne gritted her teeth at Mac's words. He'd been saying them continually over the past few days. At first she had sympathized. Everyone had. But now it was an annoying litany with no way to stop it. And truthfully, she couldn't help wishing that he *had* stayed with Battle Cry. This second incident never would have happened if he had. She ignored the plainclothes guard sitting unobtrusively on the bales of hay in the far corner of the barn, a constant reminder of her failure.

"Mr. James is really angry over what happened," Mac went on. "You know, Miss Anne, he's not happy with the care here—"

"Thank you, Mac," she said, pushing herself away from the stall door. She already knew how James felt. Or, rather, she didn't know. Angry, worried, and hurt, and determined not to show it, she said, "Battle Cry looks just fine—"

"Oh, to be sure," the little man interrupted. "But I should have stayed with him. . . ."

She came to a decision. "This is not a criticism of you, Mac, but because of what happened, Curtis will work with you."

"Oh, no!" Mac exclaimed. "Mr. James won't like it—"

"Mr. James will like it," she said firmly. "He understands the necessity, as I'm sure you will. I want someone *I* trust with that horse at all times. That's final, Mac."

She ignored his grumbles as she checked on Redman Chief, who was none the worse for wear. By sheer luck they had found a large thorn on the floor of his stall. Obviously, someone had walked by and jammed it into his flesh, counting on the combination of sudden pain in an enclosed place to make him frantic. It had, and all that same person had had to do was take advantage of the confusion. All the men had rushed into the barn, thinking it was a stallion fight. And, of course, no one had noticed who *hadn't* rushed in.

Mac babbled on, and she nodded absently until she could escape outside.

Someone was definitely out to ruin her, she thought as she emerged into the sunshine. And ruin Battle Cry too. Someone who was right here at the farm. She didn't know who to trust anymore. She even had doubts about Curtis, who had been with her from the beginning. But of all her people, he was the one she trusted the most. It was a nightmare that had to end soon.

And then there was James. Her face heated with embarrassment, as it did every time she thought of the way he had yelled at her in front of her people. How could he have done that? She had been perfectly safe. She was so angry with him, and yet she couldn't help remembering that "I love you" right in the middle of his yelling.

She caught sight of Curtis, deep in conversation with James. And not a happy conversation, judging by the glowers on their faces. Both men were barely talking to her—Curtis because she agreed to the hiring of the security firm, and James because she hadn't listened to him. Curtis could stay as mad as he liked, but James . . .

Granted, she was angry with him, but she was terrified that he had changed his mind about her. Every time she looked at him, love and need pumped through her veins like rich syrup. He had made no move toward her, though, and now he was sleeping on her office couch every night. And every night she was right upstairs in her big, lonely bed. . . .

She shook off the thought. They'd had no chance to really talk with the current chaos, and right now she had to separate the two men. Unfortunately, as bad as they were with her, they were worse with each other. She hurried over.

"Well, everyone looks fine, Curtis," she said in an overly cheerful tone, stepping between the two of them. "I've told Mac you will be with the horse at all times. He's not happy, so you'll have to—"

"I know my job," Curtis snapped.

"That's debatable," James muttered just loud enough to be heard.

"Stop it!" Anne rubbed her temple. So much for subtlety. Enough was enough. "Okay, so we have a security firm poking around that none of us wants, Curtis. We may not like it, but we can hardly complain about it. And maybe it's better this way. We're not in the protection business, and we ought to stop trying to be. We're in the horse business."

She rounded on the other man, the man who had humiliated her in front of everyone for protecting *his* horse as best she could. "And you damn well better remember that, James. Curtis and his men were doing their jobs that morning when they went after Redman Chief, just as I was when I went in the field with Battle Cry. Now, back off!"

She stormed away, furious with him. How she ever could have thought he was perfect was beyond her now.

"Are you done yelling at me?" James asked, catching up with her.

"Are you done punishing me?" she asked in return.

"I'm not punishing you—"

"And you're not talking to me either."

"I don't see you babbling away, lady," he said, running his hand through his hair in frustration. "You almost got yourself killed, Anne."

"That's a convenient excuse."

"Convenient excuse!"

"Yes. I knew exactly what I was doing, and I was in no danger. Why can't you understand that?" She glanced at him, then at the ground. Her steps unconsciously quickened. "Why not just tell me you've changed your mind about . . . me?"

"I've—" He grabbed her arm and spun her around, effectively stopping her. "What the hell are you talking about?"

"About me . . . and you." Her voice broke, and she took a deep breath to compose herself. She'd get to the truth and behave like an adult while she was doing it. "About why you have been keeping your distance, and why all this anger is an excuse to stay away. Just say it and get it over with."

"Dammit, Anne, you were the one who told me to stay away!" he exclaimed. "I yelled at you because you took unnecessary risks— "

"Very necessary risks—"

"And you scared the life out of me," he continued, ignoring her interruption. "But I am keeping my distance because you said 'Not in the house,' and I completely agree. And you haven't exactly been attacking me at every moment. You've avoided even being alone with me."

"I have not! You've barely been talking to me."

"No, I haven't!"

She stared at him. He stared at her. Then they both began to laugh. He pulled her against him, and she wrapped her arms around his waist, not caring who saw them. Under her amusement she had never felt so relieved in her life.

"Things have been so crazy," she murmured. "I just didn't know what to think."

"Neither of us have been thinking straight. We've both been under pressure with this damn mischief maker loose." He sighed. "Please, no more risks. My heart couldn't take it."

"I'll keep that in mind—when I'm taking a risk."

"Annie," he warned, then rubbed her back. "I'll get used to your job and you get used to my yelling. Agreed?"

"Agreed. As long as you don't yell at me in front of my people."

"Deal. One of the best I've ever made." His arms tightened. "At least this time there was no attempt at physical damage to Battle Cry."

She lifted her head to look at him. "But it was

real damage, James. Somehow the business with the steroids has never come out, but I don't hold much hope for this second incident. My reputation for careful breeding will be ruined. As it is, my farm is on the line."

"I know." He smiled gently. "We'll stop this before it goes any further. Whoever he is, he's either incredibly clever or stupid. I'm banking on the latter. In broad daylight like that . . . it was as if he wanted to get caught."

Anne sighed. "Fortunately, all the mares Battle Cry was in with were already in foal. By sheer luck we've avoided a breeder's worst nightmare. Now we have to wait and see if the mares were too upset by the 'excitement' and miscarry. So far they're holding."

"They'll hold." He stroked her hair. "We need a diversion, and I think I have a solution to our other problem. We need some time alone with each other, sooo . . . tonight we'll take a late tour of the farm. We'll find a cozy spot under the stars. I'll pledge my eternal love, and then you'll be all over me like cream cheese on a bagel. . . ."

"Sounds wonderful," she murmured, chuckling.

"Have you told Philip?"

"No. There hasn't been time for one thing, and I wasn't sure . . ."

"We'll both talk to him tonight."

They reluctantly separated and walked hand in hand to the house.

"It figures," James said, "that I'd have to court you in the middle of a disaster. I should have seen it coming the moment you threw up on me when you were a baby."

She grinned, feeling better for the first time in days. "I aim to please."

His smile was intimate. "And it will be my pleasure. Tonight."

"Go fish."

James sighed and rooted through the pile of cards on the kitchen table. He pulled one out and tucked it into the cards fanned in his hand.

From across the table Anne grinned wryly at him. Playing Go Fish with Philip and Lettice wasn't exactly the way he'd planned their evening, he thought as he gazed at her, seeing the longing in her expression. Still, they were spending time with Philip as a family. Maybe that was more important right now than themselves. They still had to tell Philip, and this time together could make the difference in his reaction to the news. James had to admit he was finding a special pleasure in every moment of Go Fish. He was coming to care for the boy as much as he cared about Anne.

"Got any threes?" Philip asked his great-grandmother.

The boy held his cards with a studied carelessness. He looked almost bored with the proceedings in spite of the five completed sets lying in front of him. Nobody else had any points yet. James vowed never to play poker with the kid. He'd probably lose his entire stock portfolio in the first five minutes.

"Brat," Lettice grumbled as she handed over three cards.

Philip grinned at her, placing another completed set on the table. "Now, now, Grandmother Lettice. A Kitteridge is not a sore loser."

Lettice eyed him sourly. "One Kitteridge at this

table is going to have a sore butt if he doesn't stop being a smug winner."

James looked at Anne, and both of them started laughing. Philip grinned, unrepentant, while Lettice tried to look dignified and unruffled. James admired Philip's courage with Lettice, who could make a great white shark look like a cuddly kitten at times. Losing at cards was one of them.

Suddenly he found himself the recipient of Philip's nonchalant expression. He sobered.

"Got any aces?"

"Wehll," James drawled, studying his hand. He grinned at the crossed-out hearts and A's on one of his cards. "I have one that used to be an ace. I think. It's not an ace now."

"Really, Anne," Lettice said, groaning. "This is ridiculous, playing with two decks of cards combined into one. And changing some of them into completely new cards! I'm not even sure what I have anymore. If you don't buy one decent deck of cards, then I will!"

"It's not on your list of things you can have with you while you're here," Anne replied, laughing. "Besides, this way is more fun. Right, Philip?"

"Right. Are you sure you don't have any aces?" the boy asked earnestly. "Maybe you're tired and not reading it right. I can help you. . . ."

"Nice try to get a peek at my cards, Philip," James said, chuckling. "But I'm reading just fine tonight. Go fish."

Anne set her cards down on the table, drawing his attention. She was staring at him. "Philip knows about your dyslexia."

"I told him a while back." He frowned, puzzled. "Why?"

"A while back? You told my son before me?"

He nodded, growing uneasy with her questions. She seemed upset, and he had no idea why.

She turned to her grandmother. "And you know?"

Lettice was frowning, too, clearly as bewildered as he with Anne's questions. "Of course. I've known for years, from Maida."

"*I* didn't know for years." Anne looked back at him, her eyes narrowed with anger. "I didn't know until the other day."

"It's not something I advertise," he said, hearing the defensiveness in his voice and not able to stop it. What the hell was wrong with her? She had been so damned understanding when he told her.

"All these years I thought you were perfect."

"And now you're angry that I'm not?" He should have known she'd find some excuse. Pain ripped through him.

"No, I'm angry that everyone knew before me." She leaned forward and stabbed the air with her finger. "Dammit, James. All these years you have seemed so . . . perfect. Always doing and saying the right thing. Not an imperfection anywhere. And then you—you never called after that dance. . . ."

"What dance?" Lettice asked.

They ignored her, intent on each other. "I thought I didn't measure up," she said.

"Annie," he said, realizing how he had accidentally hurt her all those years before. "It was the dyslexia. I had just been rejected because of it, and I couldn't face another rejection—especially from you."

"Believe me, I would have been thrilled to know you weren't perfect. All this time I vowed to stay away from you because . . . and I fell for you anyway."

"You didn't want to because you thought I was perfect?" he asked in astonishment.

"Yes. No." She waved her hands in the air. "It was a lot of things."

"Does this mean the game's over?" Philip asked.

"Yes," Lettice said, collecting the cards.

"It means I—" Anne took her son's hand. "I love you, Philip. And I love James, even though I'm a little angry at the moment."

"And I'm confused," James said, "but I love your mother."

"I know all about that," Philip said, smiling. "Grandmother Lettice told me the night we went to dinner. That's why we went. To help matchmakin' you 'cause you needed help to love each other and be happy." He shrugged, half embarrassed. "I like James . . . Well, it's okay with me."

Lettice shrugged in her turn, as James and Anne rounded on her. "If I waited for you two, all hell would freeze over."

"Is there anything I'm the first to know?" Anne asked the room in general.

"I doubt it," James replied, relaxing. Philip clearly approved of him, and he was extremely pleased with the thought. He stretched his arms and said as casually as possible, "I suppose we ought to check on security."

Color tinged Anne's cheeks, making her look unexpectedly shy and vulnerable. He loved knowing he could do that to his tigress.

She shrugged. "I guess it's about time."

"About."

Philip didn't ask to go along, instead becoming

busy with cleaning up an already cleaned-up kitchen. James hid a smile at his "helpfulness."

A few minutes later he was shutting the kitchen door behind him and Anne. He snapped on the flashlight, its powerful beam illuminating their path.

"Okay, now, why are you angry?" he asked as they walked along. "Besides everyone knowing before you. I'm sorry. Your opinion was the one I cared about the most, that's why it took so long to tell you."

"I don't know. It's just that my family knew something that I wish I had known from the beginning."

"It would have made a difference?"

She nodded. "Instead I had to fight the image of the man to find the man."

"Then I'm glad you didn't know. I think I would have wondered if you cared only because I did have dyslexia." He chuckled. "That would have been ironic as hell. I just wanted it not to matter."

"It doesn't matter. Only you matter."

He stopped and kissed her. Her mouth was sweet honey and summer heat. Reluctantly, very reluctantly, he lifted his head. "Let's get this damn inspection over with."

"James . . ."

Anne's head was spinning, and she felt unsteady on her feet. How he managed to do that, she didn't know. Just as long as he managed it only with her.

She felt silly now for being angry earlier back at the house. But it had suddenly hit her that if she had known, they might not have wasted so many years. James was right, though. It would have been awful to wonder if a learning disability had made her fall in love with him. Instead, it hadn't mattered. Just as it should be.

The reason for the tour surfaced through her thoughts, and she asked, "How long will the security firm be here, James?"

"As long as it takes to catch the person doing this." He squeezed her hand.

She sighed at the thought of continuing disruption. "The breeding season is almost over, only another couple of weeks are left. The two incidents with Battle Cry were directed at his breeding. Once the season stops, I have a feeling the nastiness will stop."

James shook his head. "I think things will escalate *because* the season's almost over. He'll have to achieve whatever goal he has in mind or wait another year."

Anne moaned, horrified at the idea. "Please, no."

"Agreed. What do you say about utilizing the breeding shed?" he asked as the small building became visible about a hundred yards away. "For human purposes. Very human."

"James!" she exclaimed, laughing at the notion. "You're crazy."

"I'm trying to be sexy."

"No comment."

"Well, where do you suggest?"

"This is so . . . clinical," she said, sighing. "Where's the moonlight and roses? Where are the stars and shadows? Where's the romance—"

"Shh!" He snapped off the flashlight.

"Where's the 'shh'?" she asked, astonished that he'd hushed her like that.

"Shh!" He nudged her arm and pointed toward

the breeding shed. His voice was a bare whisper. "There's someone over there."

"One of the security people?" she whispered back, peering at the shadows. She saw a vague shape flit around the building.

"I don't think so. Whoever it is, he's carrying a can. I'll go and check. Stay here, and use this on anyone except me."

"James!" she cautioned as he shoved the flashlight into her hands and slipped away from her in the darkness.

Damn that man, she thought, spinning around trying to find him. How could he yell at her for taking risks when he plunged right into trouble? And if she went after him, he'd yell at her for not listening to him . . . and if she didn't, she was terrified he might get hurt and she wouldn't know it. Hadn't he ever heard of the buddy system, for goodness' sake?

She had just started moving toward the shed when a loud "poof" filled the air. An odd orange light was barely visible from the other side of the building. She started running as an acrid odor reached her. She saw flames licking at painted wood.

Someone had set the breeding shed on fire.

"James!" she screamed, looking everywhere in an attempt to spot him. "James!"

An "oowff" erupted to her right, and she veered toward it . . . just in time to see two struggling bodies fall to the ground.

"Ouch! Dammit!"

James cursed a blue streak, as if he were going for his doctorate in vulgarism. The other man was silent, concentrating on stopping his opponent. Relief and panic washed through her. She ran over and flicked on the flashlight.

"I can't see," James shouted.

She swung the light away and turned it off, but not before she got a shocking glimpse of the other man. "It's Mac!"

"No . . . oowff . . . kidding."

Suddenly men were swarming around them, pulling James and Mac apart. Curtis motioned others toward the shed and shouted for them to start putting out the fire.

Anne threw herself into James's arms. He held her tightly.

"Dammit, Anne. You didn't stay put."

"Right. Just be grateful I didn't hit you over the head with the flashlight." She straightened away from him and faced Mac. "Why? What did I do to you, Mac?"

The older man looked broken and defeated. "I meant no harm to you personally, miss. But they were taking my boy away from me. I raised him, taught him his schools, was the first one on his back. He was mine! Mine! Not theirs to sell like a piece of meat. No one loves him like I love him, but I couldn't buy him. I always thought we'd be together, that when he was done racing we'd be put out to pasture together. But they sold him to . . . this."

"Were you . . ." She swallowed back a wave of horror. "Were you trying to kill him?"

"No!" Mac looked appalled. "I'd never hurt my boy. I thought maybe if he was useless at the breeding . . . but you found that out. After that you were extra careful with him. I thought then if I messed up his breeding line, Mr. James would move him to another farm and I might have more of a chance. You stopped that."

Suddenly everything clicked into place. Mac's continual protestations of innocence to keep anyone from suspecting him. She remembered the odd words of bitterness when he arrived, and how he had insisted that Battle Cry hated to be touched by strangers, then later told Lettice the horse was always the friendliest in the stable. They had been clues, but he had presented all of them with such ingratiation and charm, they all had been taken in by it.

"And tonight?" James asked, his voice harsh. "What did setting fire to the shed accomplish?"

"Those damn security people!" Mac spat out. "All over the place, watching me, watching everyone. And always watching my boy. I knew I had to take him away. Nothing else would work. So I set the shed . . . I'm sorry, miss, but I had to, to get everyone away so I could get my boy."

"Take him," James said to two of the security people.

The guards turned away with the old man. All the horse people were silent, knowing how easy it was to go over that edge.

Anne looked at Curtis. "Who's with Battle Cry?"

He grinned. "Safe enough with your security firm back at the barn."

"Glad you approve," James said to the man.

Curtis tilted his head. "Maybe. Put two and two together when Mac disappeared out of the barn tonight. Fire department's been called, Anne. They should be here shortly."

With that, he nodded and walked away.

"I suppose he'll never really like me," James said.

"I hope not." Anne wrapped her arms around his waist. "At least not more than as a friend. Curtis is gay. He's also better-looking than I am."

"Naaa," James said.

Anne laughed.

"I'm sorry about Mac, Anne." He shook his head. "When I think of how I insisted he take care of Battle Cry . . ."

"You didn't know. I don't think anybody picked up on the clues."

James nodded. "I refuse to feel guilty about buying Battle Cry. But looking back, it's almost easy to see that Mac was the one. Clearly, it was an inside person, yet one who didn't quite know what he was doing. And his very vocal blaming of himself for neglecting 'his boy' was too strong. He had nothing else to do but look after Battle Cry, so how could anyone get near enough to do some mischief?" James glanced toward the breeding shed, the flames already being extinguised. "Well, so much for a great idea."

She sighed. "Abstinence makes the heart grow fonder?"

"My heart couldn't get any fonder," he said in a low voice. He kissed her neck at the sensitive point just under her ear. "But abstinence stinks."

Anne burst into laughter.

By morning James had had enough. The night, to his complete disgust, had been spent with the police and the fire department. Neither Anne nor he had had a choice on turning Mac over to the police, but they both knew the man's punishment was not being with his beloved horse. They had allowed him to say good-bye to Battle Cry, but the animal had served his own brand of justice on the old man, turning away from him to his manger of straw as if he didn't exist. Mac's tears had been painful to see.

James put the thought out of his head. It was over, and Anne was safe. Battle Cry too. Time to go back to his condo . . . and his lonely bed. The couch in Anne's office was bad enough, but at least they were under the same roof. He'd have to do something.

The moment he joined her and Philip at breakfast, he knew exactly what to do.

"Marry me, Anne."

Cornflakes shot out of her mouth. He grinned as she swiped at them. "What?"

"Marry me. I want to be here with you. I love you. Marry me."

"I . . ."

Philip was grinning. "Say yes, Mom."

Anne grinned back, then turned to James. He could already see the answer in her eyes.

"Yes."

He smiled, reaching across the table to take her hand. "I love you."

"I love you." Her fingers were warm and tight around his.

"Well, it's about time!" Lettice pronounced, and walked over to the telephone.

"Grandmother, you don't have to call the papers now," Anne said.

"I'm not. My work here is done, and I'm calling for a moving van to take me back home."

"But you have only your clothes and the four things I allowed you," Anne said.

Lettice walked back over and patted her cheek.

"When was the last time you were in the guest room?"

"The guest room?"

"It's hardly four things now."

"More like forty," Philip said, giggling. "Grandmother Lettice has been bringing stuff in here when you weren't lookin'."

Lettice smiled triumphantly. "You were very impressive, child, but you've got a long way to go to beat a professional."

Anne flopped back in the chair. "That tablecloth, the brushes. That new table in the den."

"Exactly."

"Is there *anything* I know before you do?"

"That I'm marrying you," James suggested, laughing.

"Oh, I knew that too," Lettice said. "Ever since she threw up on you."

James turned to Anne. "You don't suppose . . ."

She grinned. "Naaa. I managed that one all by myself."

"The girl of my dreams."

They laughed together.

Epilogue

Anne watched the horses walk onto the track in single file. The third one shuffled along, its nose nearly touching the ground.

"Rainbow's Battle looks rarin' to go," she pronounced with great satisfaction.

"He looks ready to fall asleep!" Lettice exclaimed. "And I bet a small fortune to win!"

The others in the exclusive glass-enclosed owner's box high above the stands of the racetrack looked dubious.

"Twenty dollars is not a fortune, Lettice," James said, putting his arm around his wife. "Besides, it's his first race, so you're showing him support."

Lettice grumbled, but subsided.

Anne smiled up at her husband, knowing he was just as excited as she. Rainbow's Battle, the first of the foals born from Battle Cry out of Lollipop's Rainbow, wasn't scheduled to do much today, but she and James were hoping their two-year-old would show the beginnings of the family talent.

"Lettice Farraday, you get your fingers out of that pâté!" Anne scolded, spying her other two-year-old "playing" at the buffet table.

The child grinned and put her pâté-loaded finger in her mouth. She immediately spit the hors d'oeuvre out. "Yuck!"

"Then listen next time, my love," Anne said sweetly as the child ran over and hugged her. Little Lettice had the Kitteridge blue-green eyes and the Farraday charm. She was gorgeous. Anne felt sorry for any boys who crossed her path. Her daughter would make their lives miserable.

"I *am* brilliant," the elder Lettice commented. "I doubt you two would ever have given me a namesake without my matchmaking."

Anne's cousin Ellen groaned. So did Ellen's husband, Joe Carlini.

"She's taking credit for them too," Ellen said.

"I take credit for everyone in this room," Lettice said, giving her granddaughter the regal eye.

A chorus of groans erupted at Lettice's words.

"No, Aunt Ellen, it's true," Philip said, grinning. He was in the throes of first adolescence, his twelve-year-old body gawky at the moment. But the promise was there in his blue-green eyes and ready smile. "Grandmother Lettice moved in and everything to get Dad and Mom together."

James ruffled his son's dark hair. "You helped."

Everyone chuckled at Philip's smile of pride. Anne exchanged a wry grin with several of her relatives. If it made Lettice happy to take credit, then they would all have to live with it. Still, her "matchmaking" schemes were growing with each retelling.

"They're in the gate!" Lettice shouted.

Anne reached for James's hand and squeezed it. The race was a half-mile long, and it would be over in less than two minutes.

The buzzer sounded and the gate doors flung open. Horses shot out of the boxes. Rainbow's Battle, startled, hesitated for a second. Anne's heart sank. Races were lost in a second. And 'Bow was running dead last.

"Run, dammit!" her grandmother shouted, jumping out of her seat. She waved her arms frantically, caught up in the race. "Run, or I'll turn you into glue!"

It was as if the horse heard, because he found an opening between the pack and went through it, pounding hooves churning up the dirt. Suddenly Rainbow's Battle was in fifth place and threatening the two horses fighting it out for third.

"Easy," Anne murmured, racing with him. "Just see your way . . . that's it."

The horse gained ground with every footfall. He was passing the fourth . . . the third . . . the second . . . He was a length behind the first . . .

Everybody in the booth was up and screaming, including little Lettice, who had no idea what all the excitement was about. It was just fun. But Anne had ridden in many races, and saw the finish line looming ominously close. Rainbow's Battle was racing like a true winner, but he would have to have all the drive and skill of his sires. . . .

And then it happened. Rainbow's Battle pulled even, then sped by the other horse. He crossed the finish line a half length ahead to win. The gift had been passed on.

Anne threw herself into James's arms.

"Did you see him, Annie?" he exclaimed, spinning her around and kissing her soundly.

"No, I had my eyes closed," she said, laughing. "Battle Cry's stud fees just went through the roof."

"It wouldn't mean anything without you." He smiled down at her. "I love you, Annie Farraday, and when I get you home, I'll prove it."

"And you prove it very well." She tilted her head close and told him a little piece of news she'd been saving until the race was over. "I'm pregnant again."

Her husband's lower jaw dropped open. She grinned and pushed it closed. She kissed him. "I love you."

Lettice Kitteridge watched the couple, and smiled.

THE EDITOR'S CORNER

We've selected six LOVESWEPTs for next month that we feel sure will add to your joy and excitement as you rush into the holiday season.

The marvelously witty Billie Green leads off next month with a real sizzler, **BAD FOR EACH OTHER**, LOVESWEPT #372. Just picture yourself as lovely auburn-haired journalist Keely Durant. And imagine that your boss assigns you to interview an unbelievably attractive actor-musician, a man who makes millions of women swoon, Dylan Tate. Sounds fascinating, doesn't it? So why would the news of this assignment leave Keely on the verge of a collapse? Because five years before she and Dylan had been madly, wildly attracted to each other and had shared a white-hot love affair. Now, at their first reunion, the embers of passion glow and are quickly fanned to blazing flames, fed by sweet longing. But the haunting question remains: Is this glorious couple doomed to relive their past?

Please give a big and rousing welcome to brand-new author Joyce Anglin and her first LOVESWEPT #373, **FEELING THE FLAME**—a romance that delivers all its title promises! Joyce's hero, Mr. Tall, Dark, and Mysterious, was as charming to gorgeous Jordan Donner as he was thrilling to look at. He was also humorous. He was also supremely sexy. And, as it turned out, his name was Nicholas Estevis, and he was Jordan's new boss. Initially, she could manage to ignore his attractiveness, while vowing never to mix business with pleasure. But soon Nick shattered her defenses, claiming her body and soul. Passionate and apparently caring as he was, Jordan still suspected that love was a word only she used about their relationship. Would she ever hear him say the cherished word to her?

Sandra Chastain, that lovely lady from the land of moonlight and magnolias, seems to live and breathe
(continued)

romance. Next, in LOVESWEPT #374, **PENT-HOUSE SUITE,** Sandra is at her romantic Southern best creating two memorable lovers. At first they seem to be worlds apart in temperament. Kate Weston is a feisty gal who has vowed to fill her life with adventure upon adventure and never to stay put in one place for long. Max Sorrenson, a hunk with a bad-boy grin, has built a world for himself that is more safe than thrilling. When Kate and Max fall in love despite themselves, they make fireworks . . . while discovering that building a bridge to link their lives may be the greatest fun of all.

If ever there was a title that made me want to beg, borrow, or steal a book, it's Patt Bucheister's **ONCE BURNED, TWICE AS HOT,** LOVESWEPT #375. Rhys Jones, a good-looking, smooth operator, comes to exotic Hawaii in search of a mysterious woman. At first he doesn't guess that the strawberry blonde he bumped into is more than temptation in the flesh. She is part of what has brought him all the way from London. But more, the exquisite blonde is Lani . . . and she is as swept away by Rhys as he is by her. She soon learns that Rhys is everything she ever wanted, but will he threaten her happiness by forcing her to leave the world she loves?

Welcome back the handsome hunk who has been the subject of so many of your letters— *Kyle Surprise.* Here he comes in Deborah Smith's **SARA'S SURPRISE,** LOVESWEPT #376. Dr. Sara Scarborough saw that Kyle had gotten through the sophisticated security system that guarded her privacy. And she saw, of course, the terrible scars that he had brought back from their hellish imprisonment in Surador. Sara, too, had brought back wounds, the sort that stay buried inside the heart and mind. Demanding, determined, Kyle is soon close to Sara once more, close as they'd been in

(continued)

the prison. Yet now she has a "surprise" that could leave him breathless . . . just as breathless as the searing, elemental passion they share.

From first meeting—oops, make that impact—the lovers are charmed and charming in Judy Gill's thrilling **GOLDEN SWAN,** LOVESWEPT #377. Heroine B. J. Gray is one lady who is dynamite. Hero Cal Mixall is virile, dashing, and impossibly attracted to B.J. But suddenly, after reacting wildly to Cal's potent kisses, she realizes this is the man she's hated since she was a teenager and he'd laughed at her. Still, B.J. craves the sweet heat of him, even as she fears he'll remember the secret of her past. And Cal fears he has a job that is too tall an order: To convince B.J. to see herself as he sees her, as an alluring beauty. An unforgettable love story!

Do turn the page and enjoy our new feature that accompanies the Editor's Corner, our Fan of the Month. We think you'll enjoy getting acquainted with Patti Herwick.

As always at this season, we send you the same wishes. May your New Year be filled with all the best things in life—the company of good friends and family, peace and prosperity, and, of course, love. Warm wishes from all of us at LOVESWEPT.

Sincerely,

Carolyn Nichols

Carolyn Nichols
Editor
LOVESWEPT
Bantam Books
666 Fifth Avenue
New York, NY 10103

FAN OF THE MONTH

Patti Herwick

I first heard of LOVESWEPTs in a letter from Kay Hooper. We had been corresponding for some time when Kay told me she was going to start writing for Bantam LOVESWEPT. Naturally, since Kay was special—and still is—I was eager for the LOVESWEPTs to be published. I was hooked from then on. I read books for enjoyment. When a book comes complete with humor *and* a good story, I will buy it every time. As far as I'm concerned, LOVESWEPTs haven't ever changed. The outstanding authors that LOVESWEPT has under contract keep giving us readers better and more interesting stories. I am enchanted with the fantasy stories that Iris Johansen writes, the wonderful, happy stories that Joan Elliott Pickart writes, and, of course, Kay Hooper's. I can't say enough about Kay's work. She is a genius, her writing has gotten better and better. Every one of her books leaves me breathless. Sandra Brown is my favorite when it comes to sensual books, and I enjoy Fayrene Preston's books also. The fact that LOVESWEPTs are so innovative—with books like the Delaney series and Cherokee series—is another reason I enjoy reading LOVESWEPTs. I *like* different stories.

Now, as for me, I'm 44 years old, married, and have one grandchild. I think that I've been reading since the cradle! I like historical romances along with the LOVESWEPTs, and I probably read between 30 and 40 books a month. I became the proud owner of my own bookstore mostly because my husband said if I didn't do *something* about all my books, we were going to have to quit renting our upstairs apartment and let the books take over completely! I enjoy meeting other people who like to read, and I encourage my customers to talk about their likes and dislikes in the books. I never go *anywhere* without a book, and this has caused some problems. One time, while floating and reading happily on a swim mat in the water, I floated away. My husband got worried, searched, and when he found me and brought me back, he decided to do something so he wouldn't have the same problem again. Now he puts a soft nylon rope around the inflatable raft and *ties* it to the dock! I can only float 50 feet in any direction, but I can read to my heart's content.

I would like to thank LOVESWEPT for this wonderful honor. To have been asked to be a Fan of the Month is a memory I will treasure forever.

NEW!
Handsome Book Covers Specially Designed To Fit Loveswept Books

Our new French Calf Vinyl book covers come in a set of three great colors— royal blue, scarlet red and kachina green.

Each 7" × 9½" book cover has two deep vertical pockets, a handy sewn-in bookmark, and is soil and scratch resistant.

To order your set, use the form below.

THE DELANEY DYNASTY

Men and women whose loves an passions are so glorious
it takes many great romance novels by three bestselling
authors to tell their tempestuous stories.

THE SHAMROCK TRINITY

☐	21975	RAFE, THE MAVERICK *by Kay Hooper*	$2.95
☐	21976	YORK, THE RENEGADE *by Iris Johansen*	$2.95
☐	21977	BURKE, THE KINGPIN *by Fayrene Preston*	$2.95

THE DELANEYS OF KILLAROO

☐	21872	ADELAIDE, THE ENCHANTRESS *by Kay Hooper*	$2.75
☐	21873	MATILDA, THE ADVENTURESS *by Iris Johansen*	$2.75
☐	21874	SYDNEY, THE TEMPTRESS *by Fayrene Preston*	$2.75

THE DELANEYS: *The Untamed Years*

☐	21899	GOLDEN FLAMES *by Kay Hooper*	$3.50
☐	21898	WILD SILVER *by Iris Johansen*	$3.50
☐	21897	COPPER FIRE *by Fayrene Preston*	$3.50

Buy them at your local bookstore or use this page to order.

Bantam Books, Dept. SW7, 414 East Golf Road, Des Plaines, IL 60016

Please send me the items I have checked above. I am enclosing $_____
(please add $2.00 to cover postage and handling). Send check or money
order, no cash or C.O.D.s please.

Mr/Ms _____

Address _____

City/State _____ Zip _____

SW7–11/89

Please allow four to six weeks for delivery.
Prices and availability subject to change without notice.

Special Offer
Buy a Bantam Book
for only 50¢.

Now you can have Bantam's catalog filled with hundreds of titles plus take advantage of our unique and exciting bonus book offer. A special offer which gives you the opportunity to purchase a Bantam book for only 50¢. Here's how!

By ordering any five books at the regular price per order, you can also choose any other single book listed (up to a $5.95 value) for just 50¢. Some restrictions do apply, but for further details why not send for Bantam's catalog of titles today!

Just send us your name and address and we will send you a catalog!
